ALISTAIR M... P9-CQY-430

The Lost Salt Gift
of Blood

With an Afterword by Joyce Carol Oates

M&S

First published in 1976 by McClelland and Stewart
New Canadian Library edition 1989

Canadian Cataloguing in Publication Data

MacLeod, Alistair
The lost salt gift of blood

(New Canadian library)
Bibliography: p.

ISBN 0-7710-9969-X
I. Title.   II. Series

PS8575.L46L68 1989   C813'.54   C89-093675-7
PR9199.3.M2579L68 1989

We acknowledge the financial support of the Government of Canada through
the Book Publishing Industry Development Program for our publishing
activities. We further acknowledge the support of the Canada Council for the
Arts and the Ontario Arts Council for our publishing program.

Typesetting by Trigraph Inc.
Printed and bound in Canada

McClelland & Stewart Inc.
The Canadian Publishers
481 University Avenue
Toronto, Ontario
M5G 2E9

5 6 7 8   03 02 01 00 99

Contents

ONE

In the Fall

W E'LL JUST have to sell him," I remember my mother saying with finality. "It will be a long winter and I will be alone here with only these children to help me. Besides he eats too much and we will not have enough feed for the cattle as it is."

It is the second Saturday of November and already the sun seems to have vanished for the year. Each day dawns duller and more glowering and the waves of the grey Atlantic are sullen and almost yellow at their peaks as they pound relentlessly against the round smooth boulders that lie scattered as if by a careless giant at the base of the ever-resisting cliffs. At night, when we lie in our beds, we can hear the waves rolling in and smashing, rolling in and smashing, so relentless and regular that it is possible to count rhythmically between the thunder of each: one, two, three, four; one, two, three, four.

It is hard to realize that this is the same ocean that is the crystal blue of summer when only the thin oil-slicks left by the fishing boats or the startling whiteness of the riding seagulls mar its azure sameness. Now it is roiled and angry, and almost anguished; hurling up the brown dirty balls of scudding foam, the sticks of pulpwood from some lonely freighter, the caps of unknown men, buoys from mangled fishing nets and the inevitable bottles that contain no messages. And always also the shreds of blackened and stringy seaweed that it has ripped and torn from its

7

own lower regions, as if this is the season for self-mutilation – the pulling out of the secret, private, unseen hair.

We are in the kitchen of our house and my mother is speaking as she energetically pokes at the wood and coal within her stove. The smoke escapes, billows upward and flattens itself out against the ceiling. Whenever she speaks she does something with her hands. It is as if the private voice within her can only be liberated by some kind of physical action. She is tall and dark with high cheek-bones and brown eyes. Her hair which is very long and very black is pulled back severely and coiled in a bun at the base of her neck where it is kept in place by combs of coral.

My father is standing with his back toward us and is looking out the window to where the ocean pounds against the cliffs. His hands are clasped behind his back. He must be squeezing them together very tightly because they are almost white – especially the left. My father's left hand is larger than his right and his left arm is about three inches longer than normal. That is because he holds his stevedore's hook in his left hand when he works upon the waterfront in Halifax. His complexion is lighter than my mother's and his eyes are grey which is also the predominant colour of his thinning hair.

We have always lived on the small farm between the ocean and the coal-mining town. My father has always worked on his land in the summer and at one time he would spend his winters working within the caverns of the coal mine. Later when he could bear the underground no longer he had spent the time from November to April as an independent coal-hauler or working in his woodlot where he cut timbers for the mine roof's support. But it must have been a long time ago for I can scarcely remember a time when the mine worked steadily or a winter when he has been with us and I am almost fourteen. Now each winter he goes to Halifax but he is often a long time in going. He will stand as he does now, before the window, for perhaps a week or more and then he will be gone and we will see him only at Christmas and on the odd week-end; for he will be over two hundred miles away and the winter storms will make travelling difficult and uncertain. Once, two years ago, he came home for a weekend and the blizzard came so savagely and with such intensity that he could not return until Thursday. My mother told him he was a fool to make such a journey and that he had lost a week's wages for nothing – a week's wages that she and six children could certainly use. After that he did not come again until it was almost spring.

"It wouldn't hurt to keep him another winter," he says now, still looking out the window. "We've kept him through all of them before. He doesn't eat much now since his teeth have gone bad."

"He was of some use before," says my mother shortly and rattling the lids of her stove. "When you were home you used him in the woods or to haul coal – not that it ever got us much. These last years he's been worthless. It would be cheaper to rent a horse for the summer or per-haps even hire a tractor. We don't need a horse anymore, not even a young one, let alone one that will probably die in March after we've fed him all that time." She replaces the stove-lids – all in their proper places.

They are talking about our old horse Scott who has been with us all of my life. My father had been his driver for two winters in the underground and they had become fond of one another and in the time of the second spring, when he left the mine forever, the man had purchased the horse from the Company so that they might both come out together to see the sun and walk upon the grass. And that the horse might be saved from the blindness that would inevitably come if he remained within the deeps; the darkness that would make him like itself.

At one time he had even looked like coal, when his coat was black and shiny strong, relieved by only a single white star in the centre of his forehead; but that too was a long time ago and now he is very grey about the eyes and his legs are stiff when he first begins to walk.

"Oh, he won't die in March," says my father, "he'll be okay. You said the same thing last fall and he came through okay. Once he was on the grass again he was like a two-year-old."

For the past three or four years Scott has had heaves. I guess heaves come to horses from living too near the ocean and its dampness; like asthma comes to people, making them cough and sweat and struggle for breath. Or perhaps from eating dry and dusty hay for too many winters in the prison of a narrow stall. Perhaps from old age too. Perhaps from all of them. I don't know. Someone told my little brother David who is ten that dampening the hay would help, and last winter from early January when Scott began to cough really bad, David would take a dipper of water and sprinkle it on the hay after we'd put it in the manger. Then David would say the coughing was much better and I would say so too.

"He's not a two-year-old," says my mother shortly and begins to put on her coat before going out to feed her chickens. "He's old and useless and we're not running a rest home for retired horses. I am alone here with six children and I have plenty to do."

Long ago when my father was a coal-hauler and before he was married he would sometimes become drunk, perhaps because of his loneliness, and during a short February day and a long February night he had drunk and talked and slept inside the bootlegger's oblivious to the frozen world without until in the next morning's dehydrated despair he had staggered to the door and seen both horse and sleigh where he had left them and where there was no reason for them to be. The coal was glowing black on the sleigh beneath the fine powdered snow that seems to come even when it is coldest, seeming more to form like dew than fall like rain, and the horse was standing like a grey ghostly form in the early morning's darkness. His own black coat was covered with the hoar frost that had formed of yesterday's sweat, and tiny icicles hung from his nose.

My father could not believe that the horse had waited for him throughout the night of bitter cold, untied and unnecessary, shifting his feet on the squeaking snow, and flickering his muscles beneath the frozen harness. Before that night he had never been waited for by any living thing and he had buried his face in the hoar-frost mane and stood there quietly for a long, long time, his face in the heavy black hair and the ice beading on his cheeks.

He has told us this story many times even though it bores my mother. When he tells it David sits on his lap and says that he would have waited too, no matter how long and no matter how cold. My mother says she hopes David would have more sense.

"Well, I have called MacRae and he is to come for him today," my mother says as she puts on her coat and prepares to feed her chickens. "I wanted to get it over with while you were still here. The next thing I know you'll be gone and we'll be stuck with him for another winter. Grab the pail, James," she says to me, "come and help me feed the chickens. At least there's some point in feeding them."

"Just a minute," he says, "just a goddamn minute." He turns quickly from the window and I see his hands turn into fists and his knuckles white and cold. My mother points to the younger children and shakes her head. He is temporarily stymied because she has so often told him he must not swear before them and while he hesitates we take our pails and escape.

As we go to where the chickens are kept, the ocean waves are even higher, and the wind has risen so that we have to use our bodies to shield the pails that we carry. If we do not their contents will be scooped out and scattered wildly to the skies. It is beginning to rain and the drops are so driven by the fierceness of the wind that they ping against the galvanized sides of the pails and sting and then burn upon our cheeks.

Inside the chicken-house it is warm and acrid as the chickens press around us. They are really not chickens any more but full-grown capons which my mother has been raising all summer and will soon sell on the Christmas market. Each spring she gets day-old chicks and we feed them ground-up hardboiled eggs and chick-starter. Later we put them into outside pens and then in the fall into this house where they are fattened. They are Light Sussex which is the breed my mother favours because they are hardy and good weight-producers. They are very, very white now with red combs and black and gold glittering eyes and with a ring of startling black at the base of their white, shining necks. It is as if a white fluid had been poured over their heads and cascaded down their necks to where it suddenly and magically changed to black after exposure to the air. The opposite in colour but the same in lustre. Like piano keys.

My mother moves about them with ease and they are accustomed to her and jostle about her as she fills their troughs with mash and the warm water we have brought. Sometimes I like them and sometimes I do not. The worst part seems to be that it doesn't really matter. Before Christmas they will all be killed and dressed and then in the spring there will be another group and they will always look and act and end in the same way. It is hard to really like what you are planning to kill and almost as hard to feel dislike, and when there are many instead of one they begin to seem almost as the blueberries and strawberries we pick in summer. Just a whole lot of them to be alive in their way for a little while and then to be picked and eaten, except it seems the berries would be there anyway but the capons we are responsible for and encourage them to eat a great deal, and try our best to make them warm and healthy and strong so that we may kill them in the end. My father is always uncomfortable around them and avoids them as much as possible. My friend Henry Van Dyken says that my father feels that way because he is Scottish, and that Scotsmen are never any good at raising poultry or flowers because they think such tasks are for women and that they make a man ashamed. Henry's father is very good at raising both.

As we move about the closeness of the chicken-house the door bangs open and David is almost blown in upon us by the force of the wind and the rain. "There's a man with a big truck that's got an old bull on it," he says, "he just went in the house."

When we enter the kitchen MacRae is standing beside the table, just inside the door. My father is still at the window, although now with his back to it. It does not seem that they have said anything.

MacRae, the drover, is in his fifties. He is short and heavy-set with a red face and a cigar in the corner of his mouth. His eyes are small and bloodshot. He wears Wellington boots with his trousers tucked inside them, a broad western-style belt, and a brown suede jacket over a flannel shirt which is open at the neck exposing his reddish chest-hair. He carries a heavy stock whip in his hand and taps it against the side of his boot. Because of his short walk in the wind-driven rain his clothes are wet and now in the warmth of the kitchen they give off a steamy, strong odour that mingles uncomfortably with that of his cigar. An odour that comes of his jostling and shoving the countless frightened animals that have been carried on the back of his truck, an odour of manure and sweat and fear.

"I hear you've got an old knacker," he says now around the corner of his cigar, "might get rid of him for mink-feed if I'm lucky. The price is twenty dollars."

My father says nothing, but his eyes which seem the grey of the ocean behind him remind me of a time when the log which Scott was hauling seemed to ricochet wildly off some half-submerged obstacle, catching the man's legs beneath its onrushing force and dragging and grinding him beneath it until it smashed into a protruding stump, almost uprooting it and knocking Scott back upon his haunches. And his eyes then in their greyness had reflected fear and pain and almost a mute wonder at finding himself so painfully trapped by what seemed all too familiar.

And it seemed now that we had, all of us, conspired

against him, his wife and six children and the cigar-smoking MacRae, and that we had almost brought him to bay with his back against the ocean-scarred window so pounded by the driving rain and with all of us ringed before him. But still he says nothing although I think his mind is racing down all the possible avenues of argument, and rejecting all because he knows the devastating truth that awaits him at the end of each: "There is no need of postponing it; the truck is here and there will never be a better opportunity; you will soon be gone; he will never be any younger; the price will never be any higher; he may die this winter and we will get nothing at all; we are not running a rest home for retired horses; I am alone here with six children and I have more than enough to do; the money for his feed could be spent on your children; don't your children mean more to you than a horse; it is unfair to go and leave us here with him to care for."

Then with a nod he moves from the window and starts toward the door. "You're not . . . " begins David, but he is immediately silenced by his mother. "Be quiet," she says, "go and finish feeding the chickens," and then, as if she cannot help it, "at least there is some point in feeding them." Almost before my father stops, I know she is sorry about the last part. That she fears that she has reached for too much and perhaps even now has lost all she had before. It is like when you attempt to climb one of the almost vertical sea-washed cliffs, edging upward slowly and groping with blue-tipped fingers from one tiny crevice to the next and then seeing the tantalizing twig which you cannot resist seizing, although even as you do, you know it can be grounded in nothing for there is no vegetation there nor soil to support it and the twig is but a reject tossed up there by the sea, and even then you are tensing yourself for the painful, bruising slide that must inevitably follow. But this time for my mother, it does not. He only stops and looks at her for a moment before forcing open the door and going out into the wind. David does not move.

"I think he's going to the barn," says my mother then with surprising softness in her voice, and telling me with her eyes that I should go with him. By the time MacRae and I are outside he is already half-way to the barn; he has no hat nor coat and is walking sideways and leaning and knifing himself into the wind which blows his trousers taut against the outlines of his legs.

As MacRae and I pass the truck I cannot help but look at the bull. He is huge and old and is an Ayrshire. He is mostly white except for the almost cherry-red markings of his massive shoulders and on his neck and jowls. His heavy head is forced down almost to the truck's floor by a reinforced chain halter and by a rope that has been doubled through his nose ring and fastened to an iron bar bolted to the floor. He has tried to turn his back into the lashing wind and rain and his bulk is pressed against the truck's slatted side at an unnatural angle to his grotesquely fastened head. The floor of the truck is greasy and slippery with a mixture of the rain and his own excrement, and each time he attempts to move, his feet slide and threaten to slip from under him. He is trembling with the strain, and the muscles in his shoulders give involuntary little twitches and his eyes roll upward in their sockets. The rain mingles with his sweat and courses down his flanks in rivulets of grey.

"How'd you like to have a pecker on you like that fella," shouts MacRae into the wind. "Bet he's had his share and driven it into them little heifers a good many times. Boy you get hung like that, you'll have all them horny little girls squealen' for you to take 'em behind the bushes. No time like it with them little girls, just when the juice starts runnin' in 'em and they're finding out what it's for." He runs his tongue over his lips appreciatively and thwacks his whip against the sodden wetness of his boot.

Inside the barn it is still and sheltered from the storm. Scott is in the first stall and then there is a vacant one and then those of the cattle. My father has gone up beside Scott and is stroking his nose but saying nothing. Scott rubs his head up and down against my father's chest. Although he is old he is still strong and the force of his neck as he rubs almost lifts my father off his feet and pushes him against the wall.

"Well, no time like the present," says MacRae, as he unzips his fly and begins to urinate in the alleyway behind the stalls.

The barn is warm and close and silent, and the odour from the animals and from the hay is almost sweet. Only the sound of MacRae's urine and the faint steam that rises from it disturb the silence and the scene. "Ah sweet relief," he says rezipping his trousers and giving his knees a little bend for adjustment as he turns toward us. "Now let's see what we've got here."

He puts his back against Scott's haunches and almost heaves him across the stall before walking up beside him to where my father stands. The inspection does not take long; I suppose because not much is expected of future mink-feed. "You've got a good halter on him there," says MacRae, "I'll throw in a dollar for it, you won't be needing it anyway." My father looks at him for what seems a very long time and then almost imperceptibly nods his head. "Okay," says MacRae, "twenty-one dollars, a deal's a deal." My father takes the money, still without saying anything, opens the barn door and without looking backward walks through the rain toward his house. And I follow him because I do not know what else to do.

Within the house it is almost soundless. My mother goes to the stove and begins rinsing her teapot and moving her kettle about. Outside we hear MacRae starting the engine of his truck and we know he is going to back it against the little hill beside the barn. It will be easier to load his purchase from there. Then it is silent again, except for the hissing of the kettle which is now too hot and which someone should move to the back of the stove; but nobody does.

And then all of us are drawn with a strange fascination to the window, and, yes, the truck is backed against the little hill as we knew and MacRae is going into the barn with his whip still in his hand. In a moment he reappears leading Scott behind him.

As he steps out of the barn the horse almost stumbles but regains his balance quickly. Then the two ascend the little hill, both of them turning their faces from the driving rain. Scott stands quietly while MacRae lets down the tailgate of his truck. When the tailgate is lowered it forms a little ramp from the hill to the truck and MacRae climbs it with the halter-shank in his hand, tugging it impatiently. Scott places one foot on the ramp and we can almost hear, or perhaps I just imagine it, the hollow thump of his hoof upon the wet planking; but then he hesitates, withdraws his foot and stops. MacRae tugs at the rope but it has no effect. He tugs again. He comes half-way down the little ramp, reaches out his hand, grasps the halter itself and pulls; we can see his lips moving and he is either coaxing or cursing or both; he is facing directly into the rain now and it is streaming down his face. Scott does not move. MacRae comes down from the truck and leads Scott in a wide circle through the wet grass. He goes faster and faster, building up speed and soon both man and horse are almost running. Through the greyness of the blurring, slanting rain they look almost like a black-and-white movie that is badly out of focus. Suddenly without changing speed MacRae hurries up the ramp of the truck and the almost trotting horse follows him, until his hoof strikes the tailboard. Then he stops suddenly. As the rope jerks taut, MacRae who is now in the truck and has been carried forward by his own momentum is snapped backward; he bounces off the side of the bull, loses his footing on the slimy planking and falls into the wet filth of the truck box's floor. Almost before we can wonder if he is hurt, he is back upon his feet; his face is livid and his clothes are smeared with manure and running brown rivulets; he brings the whip, which he has somehow never relinquished even in his fall, down savagely between the eyes of Scott, who is still standing rigidly at the tailgate. Scott shakes his head as if dazed and backs off into the wet grass trailing the rope behind him.

It has all happened so rapidly that we in the window do not really know what to do, and are strangely embarrassed by finding ourselves where we are. It is almost as if we have caught ourselves and each other doing something that is shameful. Then David breaks the spell. "He is not going to go," he says, and then almost shouts, "He is just not going to go – ever. Good for him. Now that he's hit him, it's for sure. He'll never go and he'll have to stay." He rushes toward my father and throws his arms around his legs.

And then the door is jerked open and MacRae is standing there angrily with his whip still in his hand. His clothes are still soggy from his fall and the water trails from them in brown drops upon my mother's floor. His face is almost purple as he says, "Unless I get that fucken' horse on the truck in the next five minutes, the deal's off and you'll be a goddamn long time tryen' to get anybody else to pay that kinda money for the useless old cocksucker."

It is as if all of the worst things one imagines happening suddenly have. But it is not at all as you expected. And I think I begin to understand for the first time how difficult and perhaps how fearful it is to be an adult and I am suddenly and selfishly afraid not only for myself now but for what it seems I am to be. For I had somehow always thought that if one talked like that before women or small children or perhaps even certain men that the earth would open up or lightning would strike or that at least many people would scream and clap their hands over their ears in horror or that the offender if not turned to stone would certainly be beaten by a noble, clean-limbed hero. But it does not happen that way at all. All that happens is the deepening of the thunder-cloud greyness in my father's eyes and the heightening of the colour in my mother's cheeks. And I realize also with a sort of shock that in spite of Scott's refusal to go on the truck nothing has really changed. I mean not really; and that all of the facts remain awfully and simply the same: that Scott is old and that we are poor and that my father must soon go away and that he must leave us either with Scott or without him. And that it is somehow like my mother's shielding her children from 'swearing' for so many years, only to find one day that it too is there in its awful reality in spite of everything that she had wished and wanted. And even as I am thinking this my father goes by MacRae who is still standing in the ever-widening puddles of brown, seeming like some huge growth that is nourished by the foul-smelling waters that he himself has brought.

David who had released my father's legs with the entrance of MacRae makes a sort of flying tackle for them now but I intercept him and find myself saying as if from a great distance my mother's phrases in something that sounds almost like her voice, "Let's go and finish feeding the chickens." I tighten my grip on his arm and we almost have to squeeze past MacRae whose bulk is blocking the doorway and who has not yet made a motion to leave.

Out of doors my father is striding directly into the slashing rain to where Scott is standing in something like puzzlement with his back to the rain and his halter-shank dangling before him. When he sees my father approach he cocks his ears and nickers in recognition. My father who looks surprisingly slight with his wet clothes plastered to his body takes the rope in his hand and moves off with the huge horse following him eagerly. Their movement seems almost that of the small tug docking the huge ocean freighter, except that they are so individually and collectively alive. As they approach the truck's ramp, it is my father who hesitates and seems to flinch, and it is his foot which seems to recoil as it touches the planking; but on the part of Scott there is no hesitation at all; his hooves echo firmly and confidently on the strong wet wood and his head is almost pressed into the small of my father's back; he is so eager to get to wherever they are going.

He follows him as I have remembered them all of my life and imagined them even before. Following wildly through the darkened caverns of the mine in its dryness as his shoes flashed sparks from the tracks and the stone; and it its wetness with both of them up to their knees in water, feeling rather than seeing the landing of their splashing feet and with the coal cars thundering behind them with such momentum that were the horse to stumble the very cars he had set in motion would roll over him, leaving him mangled and grisly to be hauled above ground only as carrion for the wheeling gulls. And on the surface, follow-ing, in the summer's heat with the jolting haywagon and the sweat churned to froth between his legs and beneath his collar, fluttering white on the blackness of his glisten-ing coat. And in the winter, following, over the semi-frozen swamps as the snapping, whistling logs snaked behind him, grunting as he broke through the shimmering crystal ice which slashed his fetlocks and caused a scarlet trail of bloodied perforations on the whiteness of the snow. And in the winter, too, with the ton of coal upon the sleigh, following, even over the snowless stretches, driven bare by the wind, leaning low with his underside parallel and almost touching the ground, grunting, and swinging with violent jolts to the right and then to the left, moving the sleigh forward only by moving it sideways, which he had learned was the only way it would move at all.

Even as my father is knotting the rope, MacRae is hurrying past us and slamming shut the tailgate and drop-ping down the iron bolts that will hold it in its place. My father climbs over the side of the box and down as MacRae steps onto the running-board and up into the cab. The motor roars and the truck lurches forward. It leaves two broad wet tracks in the grass like the trails of two slimy, giant slugs and the smell of its exhaust hangs heavy on the air. As it takes the turn at the bottom of the lane Scott tries to turn his head and look back but the rope has been tied very short and he is unable to do so. The sheets of rain come down like so many slanted, beaded curtains making it impossible to see what we know is there, and then there is only the receding sound of the motor, the wet trails on the grass and the exhaust fumes in the air.

It is only then that I realize that David is no longer with me, but even as the question comes to the surface so also does its answer and I run toward the squawking of the chicken-house.

Within the building it is difficult to see and difficult to breathe and difficult to believe that so small a boy could wreak such havoc in so short a time. The air is thick with myriad dust particles from the disturbed floor, and bits of straw and tiny white scarlet-flecked feathers eddy and dip and swirl. The frightened capons, many of them already bloodied and mangled, attempt short and ungainly flights, often colliding with each other in mid-air. Their overfed bodies are too heavy for their weak and unused wings and they are barely able to get off the floor and flounder for a few feet before thumping down to dusty crippled landings. They are screaming with terror and their screams seem as unnatural as their flights, as if they had been terribly miscast in the most unsuitable of roles. Many of them are already lifeless and crumpled and dustied and bloodied on the floor, like sad, grey, wadded newspapers that had been used to wipe up blood. The sheen of their feathers forever gone.

In the midst of it all David moves like a small blood-spattered dervish swinging his axe in all directions and almost unknowingly, as if he were blindfolded. Dust has settled on the dampness of his face and the tears make tiny trails through its greyness, like lonely little rivers that have really nothing to water. A single tiny feather is plastered to his forehead and he is coughing and sobbing, both at the same time.

When my father appears beside me in the doorway he seems to notice for the first time that he is not alone. With a final exhausted heave he throws the axe at my father. "Cocksucker," he says in some kind of small, sad parody of MacRae, and bolts past us through the door almost colliding with my mother who now comes from out of the rain. He has had very little strength with which to throw the axe and it clatters uselessly off the wall and comes to rest against my father's boot, wet and bloodied with feathers and bits of flesh still clinging to its blade.

I am tremendously sorry for the capons, now so ruined and so useless, and for my mother and for all the time and work she has put into them for all of us. But I do not know what to do and I know not what to say.

As we leave the melancholy little building the wind cuts in from the ocean with renewed fury. It threatens to lift you off your feet and blow you to the skies and your crotch is numb and cold as your clothes are flattened hard against the front of your body, even as they tug and snap at your back in insistent, billowing balloons. Unless you turn or lower your head it is impossible to breathe for the air is blown back almost immediately into your lungs and your throat convulses and heaves. The rain is now a stinging sleet which is rapidly becoming the winter's first snow. It is impossible to see into it, and the ocean off which it rushes is lost in the swirling whiteness although it thunders and roars in its invisible nearness like the heavy bass blending with the shrieking tenor of the wind. You hear so much that you can hardly hear at all. And you are almost immobile and breathless and blind and deaf. Almost but not quite. For by turning and leaning your body and your head, you can move and breathe and see and hear a little at a time. You do not gain much but you can hang on to what little you have and your toes curl almost instinctively within your shoes as if they are trying to grasp the earth.

I stop and turn my face from the wind and look back the way I have come. My parents are there, blown together behind me. They are not moving, either, only trying to hold their place. They have turned sideways to the wind and are facing and leaning into each other with their shoulders touching, like the end-timbers of a gabled roof. My father puts his arms around my mother's waist and she does not remove them as I have always seen her do. Instead she reaches up and removes the combs of coral from the heaviness of her hair. I have never seen her hair in all its length before and it stretches out now almost parallel to the earth, its shining blackness whipped by the wind and glistening like the snow that settles and melts upon it. It surrounds and engulfs my father's head and he buries his face within its heavy darkness, and draws my mother closer toward him. I think they will stand there for a long, long time, leaning into each other and into the wind-whipped snow and with the ice freezing to their cheeks. It seems that perhaps they should be left alone so I turn and take one step and then another and move forward a little at a time. I think I will try to find David, that perhaps he may understand.

TWO

The Vastness of the Dark

ON THE twenty-eighth day of June, 1960, which is the planned day of my deliverance, I awake at exactly six A.M. to find myself on my eighteenth birthday, listening to the ringing of the bells from the Catholic church which I now attend only reluctantly on Sundays. "Well," I say to the bells and to myself, "at least tomorrow I will be free of you." And yet I do not move but lie quietly for a while looking up and through the window at the green poplar leaves rustling softly and easily in the Nova Scotian dawn.

The reason that I do not arise immediately on such a momentous day is partially due, at least, to a second sound that is very unlike the regular, majestic booming of the bells. It is the irregular and moistly rattling-rasping sound of my father's snoring which comes from the adjoining room. And although I can only hear him I can see very vividly in my mind how he must be: lying there on his back with his thinning iron-grey hair tousled upon the pillow and with his hollow cheeks and even his jet-black eyebrows rising and falling slightly with the erratic pattern of his breathing. His mouth is slightly open and there are little bubbles of saliva forming and breaking at its corners, and his left arm and perhaps even his left leg are hanging over the bed's edge and resting upon the floor. It seems, with his arm and leg like that, as if he were prepared within his sleeping consciousness for any kind of unexpected emergency that might arise; so that if and when it does he will only have to roll slightly to his left and straighten and be immediately standing. Half of his body already touches the floor in readiness.

In our home no one gets up before he does; but in a little while, I think, that too will happen. He will sort of gasp in a strangled way and the snoring will cease. Then there will be a few stealthy movements and the ill-fitting door will open and close and he will come walking through my room carrying his shoes in his left hand while at the same time trying to support his trousers and also to button and buckle them with his right. As long as I can remember he has finished dressing while walking but he does not handle buttons nor buckles so well since the dynamite stick at the little mine where he used to work ripped the first two fingers from his scarred right hand. Now the remaining fingers try to do what is expected of them: to hold, to button, to buckle, to adjust, but they do so with what seems a sort of groping uncertainty bordering on despair. As if they realized that there is now just too much for them to do even though they try as best they can.

When he comes through this room he will be walking softly so as not to awaken me and I will close my eyes and do my imitation of sleep so that he will think himself successful. After he has gone downstairs to start the fire there will be a pause and perhaps a few exploratory coughs exchanged between my mother and me in an unworded attempt to decide who is going to make the next move. If I cough it will indicate that I am awake and usually that means I will get up next and follow the route of my father downstairs. If, on the other hand, I make no sound, in a few minutes my mother also will come walking through my room. As she passes I will close my eyes a second time but I have always the feeling that it does not work for her; that unlike my father she can tell the difference between sleep which is real and that which is feigned. And I feel always dishonest about my deception. But today, I think, it will be the last time, and I want both of them down the stairs before I myself descend. For today I have private things to do which can only be done in the brief interval between the descent of my parents and the rising of my seven younger brothers and sisters.

Those brothers and sisters are now sleeping in a very different world across the hallway in two large rooms called generally "the girls' room" and "the boys' room." In the former there are my sisters and their names and ages are: Mary, 15, Judy, 14, Catherine, 12, and Bernadette, 3. In the other there are Daniel, 9, Harvey, 7, and David, 5. They live there, across the hall, in an alien but sociable world of half-suppressed giggles, impromptu pantomimes and muffled-silent pillow fights and fall to sleep in beds filled with oft-exchanged comic books and the crumbs of smuggled cookies. On "our" side of the hall it is very different. There is only one door for the two rooms and my parents, as I have said, have always to walk through my room to get to theirs. It is not a very good arrangement and at one time my father intended to cut another door from the hallway into their room and to close off the inadequate connecting door between their room and mine. But at one time he also probably planned to seal and cover the wooden beams and ribs that support the roof in all our rooms and he has not done that either. On the very coldest winter mornings you can look up and see the frost on the icy heads of the silver nails and see your breath in the coldly crystal air.

Sleeping over here on this side of the hall I have always felt very adult and separated from my younger brothers and sisters and their muffled worlds of laughter. I suppose it has something to do with the fact that I am the oldest by three years and circumstances have made me more alone. At one time each of us has slept in a crib in my parents' room and as I was the first I was not moved very far – only into the next room. Perhaps they kept me close because they were more nervous about me, and for a longer time, as they had not had much experience at that time with babies or younger children. So I have been here in this bed all by myself for as long as I can remember. The next three in our family are girls and I am separated from Daniel, the nearest boy, by an unbridgeable abyss of nine years. And by that time it seems my parents felt there was no point in either moving him in with me or me across the hall with him, as if they had somehow gotten used to hearing me breathing in the room so close to theirs and knew that I knew a great deal about them and about their habits and had been kind of backed into trusting me as if I were, perhaps, a younger brother or perhaps more intimately a friend. It is a strange and lonely thing to lie awake at night and listen to your parents making love in the next room and to be able even to count the strokes. And to know that they really do not know how much you know, but to know that they do know that you know; and not to know when the knowledge of your knowing came to them any more than they know when it came to you. And during these last four or five years lying here while the waves of embarrassed horniness roll over me, I have developed, apart from the problems of my own tumescent flesh, a sort of sympathy for the problem that must be theirs and for the awful violation of privacy that all of us represent. For it must be a very difficult thing for two people to try to have a sex life together when they know that the first product of that life is lying listening to them only a few feet away. Also, I know something else that I do not think they know I know.

I was told it by my paternal grandfather seven years ago when I was ten and he was eighty, on a spring day when, warmed by the sun, he had gone downtown and sat in a tavern most of the afternoon, drinking beer and spitting on the floor and slapping the table and his knee with the palm of his hand, his head wreathed in the pipe smoke of the mine-mutilated old men who were his friends. And as I passed the tavern's open door with my bag of papers he had hailed me as if I were some miniature taxi-cab and had said that he wished to go home. And so we had wended our way through the side streets and the back alleys, a small slightly embarrassed boy and a staggering but surprisingly erect old man who wanted me beside him but not to physically support him as that would hurt his pride.

"I am perfectly capable of walking home by myself, James," he said, looking down at me off the tip of his nose and over his walrus moustache, "no one is taking me home, I only want company. So you stay over on your side and I will stay on mine and we will just be friends going for a walk as indeed we are."

But then we had turned into an alley where he had placed his left arm against a building's brick wall and leaned, half-resting, his forehead against it while his right hand fumbled at his fly. And standing there with his head against the wall and with his shoes two feet from its base he had seemed like some strange, speaking hypotenuse from the geometry books at school and standing in the steam of his urine he had mumbled into the wall that he loved me, although he didn't often say so, and that he had loved me even before I was born.

"You know," he said, "when I learned that your mother was knocked up I was so happy I was just ashamed. And my wife was in a rage and your mother's parents were weeping and wringing their silly hands and whenever I was near them I would walk around looking at my shoes. But I think that, God forgive me, I may have even prayed for something like that and when I heard it I said, 'Well he will have to stay now and marry her because that's the kind of man he is, and he will work in my place now just as I've always wanted.' "

Then his forehead seemed to slide off his resting arm and he lurched unsteadily, almost bumping into me and seeming to see me for the first time. "Oh God," he said with a startled, frightened expression, "what a selfish old fool! What have I done now? Forget everything I said!" And he had squeezed my shoulder too tightly at first but then relaxed his grip and let his gigantic hand lie there limply all the way to his home. As soon as he entered his door, he flopped into the nearest chair and said almost on the verge of tears, "I think I told him. I think I told him." And my grandmother who was ten years younger turned on him in alarm but only asked, "What?" and he, raising both hands off his lap and letting them fall back in a sort of helpless gesture of despair said, "Oh you know, you know," as if he were very much afraid.

"Go on home James," she said to me evenly and kindly although I knew she was very angry, "and pay no attention to this old fool. He has never in all his life known when to open and close his pants or his mouth." As I turned to leave, I noticed for the first time that he had not redone his trousers after urinating in the alley and that his underwear was awry.

No one has ever mentioned it since but because one of my grandparents was so frightened and the other so angry I know that it is true because they do not react that strongly to anything that is not real. And knowing so I have never checked it further. And it is strange too with this added knowledge to lie in bed at night and to hear the actual beginnings of your brother and sisters, to almost share in it in an odd way and to know that you did not begin really in that same way or at least not in that bed. And I have imagined the back seats of the old cars I've seen in pictures, or the grassy hills behind the now torn-down dance halls or the beaches of sand beside the sea. I like to think somehow that it had been different for them at my conception and that there had been joy instead of grim release. But I suppose we, all of us, like to think of ourselves as children of love rather than of necessity. That we have come about because there was a feeling of peace and well-being before the erection rather than its being the other way around. But of course I may be as wrong about that as I am about many things and perhaps I do not know what they feel now anymore than what they might have felt then.

But after today, I will probably not have to think about it anymore. For today I leave behind this grimy Cape

Breton coal-mining town whose prisoner I have been for all of my life. And I have decided that almost any place must be better than this one with its worn-out mines and smoke-black houses; and the feeling has been building within me for the last few years. It seems to have come almost with the first waves of sexual desire and with it to have grown stronger and stronger with the passing months and years. For I must not become as my father whom I now hear banging the stove-lids below me as if there were some desperate rush about it all and some place that he must be in a very short time. Only to go nowhere. And I must not be as my grandfather who is now an almost senile old man, nearing ninety, who sits by the window all day saying his prayers and who in his moments of clarity remembers mostly his conquests over coal, and recounts tales of how straight were the timbers he and my father erected in the now caved-in underground drifts of twenty-five years ago when he was sixty-two and my father twenty-five and I not yet conceived.

It is a long, long time since my grandfather has worked and all the big mines he worked in and which he so romanticizes now are closed. And my father has not worked since early March, and his presence in a house where he does not want to be breeds a tension in us all that is heightened now since school is closed and we are all home and forced in upon ourselves. And as he moves about on this morning, banging stove-lids, pretending it is important that he does so, that he is wanted somewhere soon and therefore must make this noisy rush, I feel myself separated from him by a wide and variegated gulf and very far away from the man, who, shortly after he became my father, would take me for rides upon his shoulders to buy ice-cream at the drugstore, to see the baseball games I did not understand, or into the open fields to pat the pit-horses and be placed upon their broad and gentle backs. As we would approach the horses he would speak softly to them so that they might know where we were and be unafraid when he finally placed his hand upon them, for all of them were blind. They had been so long in the darkness of the mine that their eyes did not know the light, and the darkness of their labour had become that of their lives.

But now my father does not do such things with his younger children even as he no longer works. And he is older and greyer and apart from the missing fingers on his right hand, there is a scar from a broken bit that begins at his hairline and runs like violent lightning down the right side of his face and at night I can hear him coughing and wheezing from the rock dust on his lungs. And perhaps that coughing means that because he has worked in bad mines with bad air these last few years he will not live so very much longer. And perhaps my brothers and sisters across the hall will never hear him, when they are eighteen, rattling the stove-lids as I do now.

And as I lie here now on my back for the last time, I think of when I lay on my stomach in the underground for the first time with him there beside me in the small bootleg mine which ran beneath the sea and in which he had been working since the previous January. I had joined him at the end of the school year for a few short weeks before the little mine finally closed and I had been rather surprisingly proud to work there and my grandfather in one of his clearer moments said, "Once you start it takes a hold of you, once you drink underground water, you will always come back to drink some more. The water gets in your blood. It is in all of our blood. We have been working in the mines here since 1873."

The little mine paid very low wages and was poorly equipped and ventilated and since it was itself illegal there were no safety regulations. And I had thought, that first day, that I might die as we lay on our stomachs on the broken shale and on the lumps of coal while the water seeped around us and into us and chilled us with unflagging constancy whenever we ceased our mole-like movements. It was a very narrow little seam that we attacked, first with our drilling steels and bits, and then with our dynamite, and finally with our picks and shovels. And there was scarcely thirty-six inches of headroom where we sprawled, my father shovelling over his shoulders like the machine he had almost become while I tried to do what I was told and to be unafraid of the roof coming in or of the rats that brushed my face, or of the water that numbed my legs, my stomach and my testicles or of the fact that at times I could not breathe because the powder-heavy air was so foul and had been breathed before.

And I was aware once of the whistling wind of movement beside me and over me and saw by the light of my lamp the gigantic pipe-wrench of my father describing an arc over me and landing with a squealing crunch an arm's length before me; and then I saw the rat, lying on its back and inches from my eyes. Its head was splattered on the coal and on the wrench and it was still squeaking while a dying stream of yellow urine trickled down between its convulsively jerking legs. And then my father released the wrench and seizing the not quite dead rat by the tail hurled it savagely back over his shoulder so that the thud of its body could be heard behind us as it bounced off the wall and then splashed into the water. "You dirty son of a bitch," he said between clenched teeth and wiped the back of the wrench against the rocky wall. And we lay there then for a while without moving, chilled together in the dampness and the dark.

And now, strangely enough, I do not know if that is what I hate and so must leave, or if it is the fact that now there is not even that mine, awful as it was, to go to, and perhaps it is better to have a place to go to that you hate than to have no place at all. And it is the latter which makes my father now increasingly tense and nervous because he has always used his body as if it were a car with its accelerator always to the floor and now as it becomes more scarred and wasted, he can only use it for sex or taut too-rapid walks along the seashore or back into the hills; and when everything else fails he will try to numb himself with rum and his friends will bring him home in the evenings and dump him with his legs buckling beneath him, inside his kitchen door. And my mother and I will half carry and half drag him through the dining room to the base of the stairs and up the fourteen steps, counting them to ourselves, one by one. We do not always get that far; once he drove his left fist through the glass of the dining room window and I wrestled with him back and forth across the floor while the wildly swinging and still-clenched fist flashed and flecked its scarlet blood upon the floor and the wallpaper and the curtains and the dishes and the foolish sad dolls and colouring books and *Great Expectations* which lay upon the table. And when he was subdued and the fist became a hand we had to ask him politely to clench it again so that the wounds would reopen while the screaming iodine was poured over and into them and the tweezers probed for the flashing slivers of glass. And we had prayed then, he included, that no tendons were damaged and that no infection would set in because it was the only good hand that he had and all of us rode upon it as perilous passengers on an unpredictably violent sea.

Sometimes when he drinks so heavily my mother and I cannot always get him to his bed and leave him instead on mine, trying to undress him as best we can, amidst his flailing arms and legs and shouted obscenities, hoping at least to get his shoes, and loosen his collar and belt and trousers. And during the nights that follow such days I lie rigid beside him, trying to overcome the nausea caused by the sticky, sweet stench of the rum and listening to the sleep-talker's mumbled, incoherent words, his uneven snoring, and the frightening catches in his breathing caused by the phlegm within his throat. Sometimes he will swing out unexpectedly with either hand and once his forearm landed across my nose with such force that the blood and tears welled to the surface simultaneously and I had to stuff the bedclothes into my mouth to stifle the cry that rose upon my lips.

But yet it seems that all storms subside first into gusts and then into calm and perhaps without storms and gusts we might never have any calm, or perhaps having it we would not recognize it for what it is; and so when he awakens at one or two A.M. and lies there quietly in the dark it is the most peaceful of all times, like the quiet of the sea, and it is only then that I catch glimpses of the man who took me for the rides upon his shoulders. And I arise and go down the stairs as silently as I can, through the sleeping house, and fetch the milk which soothes the thickness of his tongue and the parched and fevered dryness of his throat and he says "Thank you," and that he is sorry, and I say that it is all right and that there is really nothing to be sorry for. And he says that he is sorry that he has acted the way he has and that he is sorry he has been able to give me so little but if he cannot give he will try very hard not to take. And that I am free and owe my parents nothing. That in itself is perhaps quite a lot to give, for many people like myself go to work very young here or did when there was work to go to and not everyone gets into high school or out of it. And perhaps even the completion of high school is the gift that he has given me along with that of life.

But that is also now ended, I think, the life here and the high school and the thought jolts me into the realization that I have somehow been half-dozing, for although I think I clearly remember everything, my mother has obviously already passed through this room for now I hear her moving about downstairs preparing breakfast. I am rather grateful that at least I have not had to pretend to be asleep on this the last of all these days.

Moving now as quickly as I can, I remove from beneath the mattress the battered old packsack that was my father's in earlier, younger days. "Would it be all right if I use that old packsack sometime?" I had asked as casually as possible some months before, trying to make my plans for it sound like some weary camping expedition. "Sure," he had said in an even non-committal fashion.

Now I pack it quietly, checking with my ball-point pen the items that I have listed on the back of the envelope kept beneath my pillow. Four pairs of underwear, five pairs of socks, two pairs of pants, four shirts, one towel, some handkerchiefs, a gabardine jacket, a plastic raincoat and a shaving set. The latter is the only item that is new and unused and is the cheapest that Gillette manufactures. Up until this time I have always used my father's razor which is battered and verdigris green from years of use. I have used it for some years now – more often, at times, than my questionable beard demanded.

As I move down the stairs there is still no movement from the two larger rooms across the hall and for this I am most grateful. I do not really know how to say good-bye as I have never before said it to anyone and because I am uncertain I wish to say it now to as few as possible. Who knows, though, perhaps I may even be rather good at it. I lay the packsack down on the second stair from the bottom where it is not awfully visible and walk into the kitchen. My mother is busy at her stove and my father is standing with his back to the room looking through the window over a view of slate-grey slag heaps and ruined skeletal mine tipples and out toward the rolling sea. They are not greatly surprised to see me as it is often like this, just the three of us in the quiet early morning. But today I cannot afford to be casual and I must say what must be said in the short space of time occupied by only the three of us. "I think I'll go away today," I say, trying to sound as offhand as possible. Only a slight change in the rhythm of my mother's poking at the stove indicates that she has heard me, and my father still stands looking through the window out to sea. "I think I'll go right now," I add, my voice sort of trailing off, "before the others get up it will be easier that way."

My mother moves the kettle, which has started to boil, toward the back of the stove, as if stalling for time, then she turns and says, "Where will you go? To Blind River?"

Her response is so little like that which I anticipated

that I feel strangely numb. For I had somehow expected her to be greatly surprised, astounded, astonished, and she is none of these. And her mention of Blind River, the centre of Northern Ontario's uranium mines, is something and someplace that I had never even thought of. It is as if my mother had not only known that I was to leave but had even planned my route and final destination. I am reminded of my reading in school of the way Charles Dickens felt about the blacking factory and his mother's being so fully in favour of it. In favour of a life for him which he considered so terrible and so far beneath his imagined destiny.

My father turns from the window and says, "You are only eighteen today, perhaps you could wait awhile. Something might turn up." But within his eyes I see no strong commitment to his words and I know he feels that waiting is at best weary and at worst hopeless. This also makes me somehow rather disappointed and angry as I had thought somehow my parents would cling to me in a kind of desperate fashion and I would have to be very firm and strong.

"What is there to wait for?" I say, asking a question that is useless and to which I know the all too obvious answer. "Why do you want me to stay here?"

"You misunderstand," says my father, "you are free to go if you want to. We are not forcing you or asking you to do anything. I am only saying that you do not *have* to go now."

But suddenly it becomes very important that I *do* go now, because it seems things cannot help but get worse. So I say, "Good-bye. I will write but it will not be from Blind River." I add the last as an almost unconscious little gibe at my mother.

I go and retrieve my packsack and then pass back through the house, out the door and even through the little gate. My parents follow me to the gate. My mother says, "I was planning a cake for today . . . " and then stops uncertainly, her sentence left hanging in the early morning air. She is trying to make amends for her earlier statement and rather desperately gropes her way back to the fact of my birthday. My father says, "Perhaps you should go over home. They may not be there if and when you come again."

It is but a half block to "over home," the house of my father's parents, who have always been there as long as I can remember and who have always provided a sort of haven for all of us through all our little storms and my father's statement that they will not be there forever is an intimation of something that I have never really considered before. So now I move with a sort of apprehension over the ashes and cinder-filled pot-holes of the tired street toward the old house blackened with the coal dust of generations. It is as yet hardly seven A.M. and it is as if I am some early morning milkman moving from one house to another to leave good-byes instead of bottles beside such quiet doors.

Inside my grandparents' house, my grandfather sits puffing his pipe by the window, while passing the beads of his rosary through fingers which are gnarled and have been broken more times than he can remember. He has been going deaf for some time and he does not turn his head when the door closes behind me. I decide that I will not start with him because it will mean shouting and repetition and I am not sure I will be able to handle that. My grandmother, like my mother, is busy at her stove. She is tall and white-haired and although approaching eighty she is still physically imposing. She has powerful, almost masculine hands and has always been a big-boned person without ever having been heavy or ever having any difficulty with her legs. She still moves swiftly and easily and her eyesight and hearing are perfect.

"I am going away today," I say as simply as I can.

She pokes with renewed energy at her stove and then answers: "It is just as well. There is nothing for one to do here anyway. There was never anything for one to do here."

She has always spoken with the Gaelic inflection of her youth and in that detached third-person form which I had long ago suggested that she modernize.

"Come here James," she says and takes me into her pantry, where with surprising agility she climbs up on a chair and takes from the cupboard's top shelf a huge cracked and ancient sugar bowl. Within it there are dusty picture postcards, some faded yellow payslips which seem ready to disintegrate at the touch, and two yellowed letters tied together with a shoelace. The locations on the pay-slips and on the postcards leap at me across a gulf of dust and years: Springhill, Scranton, Wilkes-Barre, Yellow-knife, Britannia Beach, Butte, Virginia City, Escanaba, Sudbury, Whitehorse, Drumheller, Harlan, Ky., Elkins, W. Va., Fernie, B.C., Trinidad, Colo. – coal and gold, copper and lead, gold and iron, nickel and gold and coal. East and West and North and South. Mementoes and messages from places that I so young and my grandmother so old have never seen.

"Your father was under the ground in all those places," she says half-angrily, "the same way he was under the ground here before he left and under it after he came back. It seems we will be underground long enough when we are dead without seeking it out while we are still alive."

"But still," she says after a quiet pause and in a sober tone, "it was what he was good at and wanted to do. It was just not what I wanted him to do, or at least I did not want him to do it here."

She unties the shoelace and shows me the two letters. The first is dated March 12, 1938, and addressed General Delivery, Kellogg, Idaho: "I am getting old now and I would like very much if you would come back and take my working place at the mine. The seam is good for years yet. No one has been killed for some time now. It is getting better. The weather is mild and we are all fine. Don't bother writing. Just come. We will be waiting for you. Your fond father."

The second bears the same date and is also addressed

General Delivery, Kellogg, Idaho: "Don't listen to him. If you return here you will never get out and this is no place to lead one's life. They say the seam will be finished in another few years. Love, Mother."

I have never seen my grandfather's handwriting before and for some reason, although I knew he read, I had always thought him unable to write. Perhaps, I think now, it is because his hands have been so broken and mis-shapen; and with increasing age, hard to control for such a fine task as writing.

The letters are written with the same broad-nibbed pen in an ink which is of a blackness that I have never seen and somehow these letters now seem like a strangely old and incompatible married couple, each cancelling out the other's desires while bound together by a single worn and dusty lace.

I go out of the pantry and to the window where my grandfather sits. "I am going away today," I shout, leaning over him.

"Oh yes," he says in a neutral tone of voice, while continuing to look out the window and finger his rosary. He does not move and the pipe smoke curls upward from his pipe which is clenched between his worn and strongly stained teeth. Lately he has taken to saying, "Oh yes," to almost everything as a means of concealing his deafness and now I do not know if he has really heard me or is merely giving what seems a standard and safe response to all of the things he hears but partially if at all. I do not feel that I can say it again without my voice breaking and so I turn away. At the door I find that he has shuffled behind me.

"Don't forget to come back James," he says, "it's the only way you'll be content. Once you drink underground water it becomes a part of you like the blood a man puts into a woman. It changes her forever and never goes away. There's always a part of him running there deep inside her. It's what will wake you up at night and never ever leave you alone."

Because he knows how much my grandmother is opposed to what he says he has tried to whisper to me. But he is so deaf that he can hardly hear his own voice and he has almost shouted in the way deaf people do; his voice seems to echo and bounce off the walls of his house and to escape out into the sunshot morning air. I offer him my hand to shake and find it almost crushed in the crooked broken force of his. I can feel the awful power of his oddly misshapen fingers, his splayed and flattened too broad thumb, the ridges of the toughened, blackened scars and the abnormally large knobs that are his twisted misplaced knuckles. And I have a feeling for a terrible moment that I may never ever get away or be again released. But he finally relaxes and I feel that I am free.

Even pot-holed streets are lonely ones when you think you may not see them again for a very long time or perhaps forever. And I travel now mostly the back streets because I am conspicuous with my packsack and I do not want any more conversations or attempted and failed and futile explanations. At the outskirts of the town a coal truck stops for me and we travel for twenty-five miles along the shoreline of the sea. The truck makes so much noise and rides so roughly that conversation with the driver is impossible and I am very grateful for the noisy silence in which we are encased.

By noon after a succession of short rides in a series of oddly assorted vehicles I am finally across the Strait of Canso, off Cape Breton Island and at last upon my way. It is only when I have left the Island that I can feel free to assume my new identity which I don like carefully preserved new clothes taken from within their pristine wrappings. It assumes that I am from Vancouver which is as far away as I can imagine.

I have been somehow apprehensive about even getting off Cape Breton Island, as if at the last moment it might extend gigantic tentacles, or huge monstrous hands like my grandfather's to seize and hold me back. Now as I finally set foot on the mainland I look across at the heightened mount that is Cape Breton now, rising mistily out of the greenness and the white-capped blueness of the sea.

My first ride on the mainland is offered by three Negroes in a battered blue Dodge pickup truck that bears the information "Rayfield Clyke, Lincolnville, N.S., Light Trucking" on its side. They say they are going the approximately eighty miles to New Glasgow and will take me if I wish. They will not go very fast, they say, because their truck is old and I might get a better ride if I choose to wait. On the other hand, the driver says, I will at least be moving and I will get there sooner or later. Anytime I am sick of it and want to stop I can bang on the roof of the cab. They would take me in the cab but it is illegal to have four men in the cab of a commercial vehicle and they do not want any trouble with the police. I climb into the back and sit on the worn spare tire and the truck moves on. By now the sun is fairly high and when I remove the packsack from my shoulders I can feel although I cannot see the two broad bands of perspiration traced and crossing upon my back. I realize now that I am very hungry and have eaten nothing since last evening's supper.

In New Glasgow I am let off at a small gas station and my Negro benefactors point out the shortest route to the western outskirts of the town. It leads through cluttered back streets where the scent of the greasy hamburgers reeks out of the doors of the little lunch-counters with their overloud juke-boxes; simultaneously pushing Elvis Presley and the rancid odours of the badly cooked food through the half open doors. I would like to stop but somehow there is a desperate sense of urgency now as if each of the cars on the one-way street is bound for a magical destination and I feel that should I stop for even a moment's hamburger I might miss the one ride that is worthwhile. The sweat is running down my forehead now and stings my eyes and I know the two dark patches of perspiration upon my back and beneath the straps are very wide.

The sun seems at its highest when the heavy red car pulls over to the highway's gravelled shoulder and its driver leans over to unlock the door on the passenger side. He is a very heavy man of about fifty with a red perspiring face and a brown cowlick of hair plastered down upon his damply glistening forehead. His coat is thrown across the back of the seat and his shirt pocket contains one of those plastic shields bristling with pens and pencils. The collar of the shirt is open and his tie is loosened and awry; his belt is also undone, as is the button at the waistband of his trousers. His pants are grey and although stretched tautly over his enormous thighs they still appear as damply wrinkled. Through his white shirt the sweat is showing darkly under his armpits and also in large blotches on his back which are visible when he leans forward. His hands seem very white and disproportionately small.

As we move off down the shimmering highway with its mesmerizing white line, he takes a soiled handkerchief that has been lying on the seat beside him and wipes the wet palms of his hands and also the glistening wet blackness of the steering wheel.

"Boy, it sure is hot," he says, "hotter'n a whore in hell."

"Yes," I say, "it sure is. It really is."

"Dirty little town back there," he says, "you can spend a week there just driving through."

"Yes, it isn't much."

"Just travelling through?"

"Yes, I'm going back to Vancouver."

"You got a whole lot of road ahead of you boy, a whole lot of road. I never been to Vancouver, never west of Toronto. Been trying to get my company to send me west for a long while now but they always send me down here. Three or four times a year. Weather's always miserable. Hotter'n hell like this here or in the winter cold enough to freeze the balls off a brass monkey." He beats out a salvo of hornblasts at a teenage girl who is standing uncertainly by the roadside.

Although the windows of the car are open, it is very hot

and the redness of the car seems to intensify the feeling and sense of heat. All afternoon the road curves and winds ahead of us like a bucking, shimmering snake with a dirty white streak running down its back. We seem to ride its dips and bends like captive passengers on a roller-coaster, leaning our bodies into the curves, and bracing our feet against the tension of the floorboards. My stomach vanishes as we hurtle into the sudden unexpected troughs and returns as quickly as we emerge to continue our twists and turns. Insects ping and splatter against the windshield and are transformed into yellow splotches. The tires hiss on the superheated asphalt and seem almost to leave tracks. I can feel my clothes sticking to me, to my legs and thighs and back. On my companion's shirt the blotches of sweat are larger and more plentiful. Leaning his neck and shoulders back against the seat he lifts his heavy body from the sweat-stained upholstery and thrusts his right hand through his opened trousers and deep into his crotch. "Let a little air in there," he says, as he manoeuvres his genitals, "must be an Indian made this underwear, it keeps creeping up on me."

All afternoon as we travel we talk or rather he talks and I listen which I really do not mind. I have never really met anyone like him before. The talk is of his business (so much salary, so much commission plus other 'deals' on the side), of his boss (a dumb bastard who is lucky he has good men on the road), of his family (a wife, one son and one daughter, one of each is enough), of sex (he can't get enough of it and will be after it until he dies), of Toronto (it is getting bigger every day and it is not like it used to be), of taxes (they keep getting higher and it doesn't pay a man to keep up his property, also too many Federal giveaways). He goes on and on. I have never listened to anyone like him before. He seems so confident and sure of everything. It is as if he knows that he knows everything and is on top of everything and he seems never to have to hesitate nor stop nor run down nor even to think; as if he were a juke-box fed from some mysterious source by an inexhaustible supply of nickels, dimes and quarters.

The towns and villages and train stations speed by. Fast and hot; Truro, Glenholme and Wentworth and Oxford. We are almost out of Nova Scotia with scarcely thirty miles of it ahead according to my companion. We are almost at the New Brunswick border. I am again in a stage of something like exhausted relief as I approach yet another boundary over which I can escape and leave so much behind. It is the feeling I originally had on leaving Cape Breton only now it has been heavied and dulled by the journey of the day. For it has been long and hot and exhausting.

Suddenly the road veers to the left and no longer hooks and curves but extends up and away from us into a long, long hill, the top of which we can see almost a half mile away. Houses appear on either side as we begin the climb and then there are more and more of them strung out loosely along the road.

My companion blasts out a rhythm of hornblasts at a young girl and her mother who are stretching up on their tiptoes to hang some washing on a clothesline. There is a basket of newly washed clothes on the ground between them and their hands are busy on the line. They have some clothespins in their teeth so they will not have to bend to reach them and lose their handhold on the line.

"If I had my way, they'd have something better'n that in their mouths," he says, "wouldn't mind resting my balls on the young one's chin for the second round."

He has been looking at them quite closely and the car's tires rattle in the roadside gravel before he pulls it back to the quiet of the pavement.

The houses are closer together now and more blackened and the yards are filled with children and bicycles and dogs. As we move toward what seems to be the main intersection I am aware of the hurrying women in their kerchiefs, and the boys with their bags of papers and baseball gloves and the men sitting or squatting on their heels in tight little compact knots. There are other men who neither sit nor squat but lean against the buildings or rest upon canes or crutches or stand awkwardly on artificial limbs. They are the old and the crippled. The faces of all of them are gaunt and sallow as if they had been allowed to see the sun only recently, when it was already too late for it to do them any good.

"Springhill is a hell of a place," says the man beside me, "unless you want to get laid. It's one of the best there is for that. Lots of mine accidents here and the men killed off. Women used to getting it all the time. Mining towns are always like this. Look at all the kids. This here little province of Nova Scotia leads the country in illegitimacy. They don't give a damn."

The mention of the name Springhill and the realization that this is where I have come is more of a shock than I would ever have imagined. As if in spite of signposts and geography and knowing it was "there," I have never thought of it as ever being "here."

And I remember November 1956: the old cars, mud-splattered by the land and rusted by the moisture of the sea, parked outside our house with their motors running. Waiting for the all-night journey to Springhill which seemed to me then, in my fourteenth year, so very far away and more a name than even a place. Waiting for the lunches my mother packed in wax paper and in newspaper and the thermos bottles of coffee and tea, and waiting for my father and the same packsack which now on this sweating day accompanies me. Only then it was filled with the miners' clothes he would need for the rescue that they hoped they might perform. The permanently blackened underwear, the heavy woollen socks, the boots with the steel-reinforced toes, the blackened, sweat-stained miner's belt which sagged on the side that carried his lamp, the crescent wrench, the dried and dustied water-bag, trousers and gloves and the hard hat chipped and dented and broken by the years of falling rock.

And all of that night my grandfather with his best ear

held to the tiny radio for news of the buried men and of their rescuers. And at school the teachers taking up collections in all of the class-rooms and writing in large letters on the blackboard, "Springhill Miners' Relief Fund, Springhill, N.S." which was where we were sending the money, and I remember also my sisters' reluctance at giving up their hoarded nickels, dimes and quarters because noble causes and death do not mean very much when you are eleven, ten and eight and it is difficult to comprehend how children you have never known may never see their fathers any more, not walking through the door nor perhaps even being carried through the door in the heavy coffins for the last and final look. Other people's buried fathers are very strange and far away but licorice and movie matinees are very close and real.

"Yeah," says the voice beside me, "I was in here six months ago and got this little, round woman. Really giving it to her, pumping away and all of a sudden she starts kind of crying and calling me by this guy's name I never heard of. Must have been her dead husband or something. Kind of scared the hell out of me. Felt like a goddamn ghost or something. Almost lost my rod. Might have too but I was almost ready to shoot it into her."

We are downtown now and it is late afternoon in the period before the coming of the evening. The sun is no longer as fierce as it was earlier and it slants off the blackened buildings, many of which are shells bleak and fire-gutted and austere. A Negro woman with two light-skinned little boys crosses the street before us. She is carrying a bag of groceries and the little boys have each an opened sixteen-ounce bottle of Pepsi-Cola. They put their hands over the bottles' mouths and shake them vigorously to make the contents fizz.

"Lots of people around here marry niggers," says the voice. "Guess they're so black underground they can't tell the difference in the light. All the same in the dark as the fellow says. Had an explosion here a few years ago and some guys trapped down there, I dunno how long. Eaten the lunches of the dead guys and the bark off the timbers and drinking one another's piss. Some guy in Georgia offered the ones they got out a trip down there but there was a nigger in the bunch so he said he couldn't take him. Then the rest wouldn't go. Damned if I'd lose a trip to Georgia because of a single nigger that worked for the same company. Like I say, I'm old enough to be your father or even your grandfather and I haven't even been to Vancouver."

It is 1958 that he is talking about now and it is much clearer in my mind than 1956 which is perhaps the difference between being fourteen and sixteen when something happens in your life. A series of facts or near facts that I did not even realize I possessed flash now in succession upon my mind: the explosion in 1958 occurred on a Thursday as did the one in 1956; Cumberland No. 2 at the time of the explosion was the deepest coal mine in North America; in 1891, 125 men were killed in that same mine; that 174 men went down to work that 1958 evening; that most were feared lost; that 18 were found alive after being buried beneath 1,000 tons of rock for more than a week; that Cumberland No. 2 once employed 900 men and now employs none.

And I remember again the cars before our house with their motors running, and the lunches and the equipment and the waiting of the week: the school collections, my grandfather with his radio, this time the added reality of a T.V. at a neighbour's house; and the quietness of our muted lives, our footsteps without sound. And then the return of my father and the haunted greyness of his face and after the younger children were in bed the quiet and hushed conversations of seeping gas and lack of oxygen and the wild and belching smoke and flames of the subterranean fires nourished there by the everlasting seams of the dark and diamond coal. And also of the finding of the remains of men flattened and crushed if they had died beneath the downrushing roofs of rock or if they had been blown apart by the explosion itself, transformed into forever lost and irredeemable pieces of themselves; hands and feet and blown-away faces and reproductive organs and severed ropes of intestines festooning the twisted pipes and spikes like grotesque Christmas-tree loops and chunks of hair-clinging flesh. Men transformed into grisly jig-saw puzzles that could never more be solved.

"I don't know what the people do around here now," says the voice at my side. "They should get out and work like the rest of us. The Government tries to resettle them but they won't stay in a place like Toronto. They always come back to their graveyards like dogs around a bitch in heat. They have no guts."

The red car has stopped now before what I am sure is this small town's only drugstore. "Maybe we'll stop here for a while," he says. "I've just about had it and need something else. All work and no play, you know. I'm going in here for a minute first to try my luck. As the fellow says, an ounce of prevention beats a pound of cure."

As he closes the door he says, "Maybe later you'd like to come along. There's always some left over."

The reality of where I am and of what I think he is going to do seems now to press down upon me as if it were the pressure of the caving-in roof which was so recently within my thoughts. Although it is still hot I roll up the windows of the car. The people on the street regard me casually in this car of too bright red which bears Ontario licence plates. And I recognize now upon their faces a look that I have seen upon my grandfather's face and on the faces of hundreds of the people from my past and even on my own when seeing it reflected from the mirrors and windows of such a car as this. For it is as if I am not part of their lives at all but am only here in a sort of movable red and glass showcase, that has come for a while to their private anguish-ridden streets and will soon roll on and leave them the same as before my coming; part of a movement that passes through their lives but does not really touch them. Like flotsam on yet another uninteresting river which flows through their permanent banks and is bound for some invisible destination around a bend where they have never been and cannot go. Their glances have summed me up and dismissed me as casually as that. "What can he know of our near deaths and pain and who lies buried in our graves?"

And I am overwhelmed now by the awfulness of over-simplification. For I realize that not only have I been guilty of it through this long and burning day but also through most of my yet young life and it is only now that I am doubly its victim that I begin vaguely to understand. For I had somehow thought that "going away" was but a physical thing. And that it had only to do with movement and with labels like the silly "Vancouver" that I had glibly rolled from off my tongue; or with the crossing of bodies of water or with the boundaries of borders. And because my father had told me I was "free" I had foolishly felt that it was really so. Just like that. And I realize now that the older people of my past are more complicated than perhaps I had ever thought. And that there are distinctions between my sentimental, romantic grandfather and his love for coal, and my stern and practical grandmother and her hatred of it; and my quietly strong but passive mother and the soaring extremes of my father's passionate violence and the quiet power of his love. They are all so different. But yet they have somehow endured and given me the only life I know for all these eighteen years. Their lives flowing into mine and mine from out of theirs. Different but somehow more similar than I had ever thought. Perhaps it is possible I think now to be both and yet to see only the one. For the man in whose glassed-in car I now sit sees only similarity. For him the people of this multi-scarred little town are reduced to but a few phrases and the act of sexual intercourse. They are only so many identical goldfish leading identical, incomprehensible lives within the glass prison of their bowl. And the people on the street view me behind my own glass in much the same way and it is the way that I have looked at others in their "foreign licence" cars and it is the kind of

judgement that I myself have made. And yet it seems that
neither these people nor this man are in any way unkind
and not to understand does not necessarily mean that one
is cruel. But one should at least be honest. And perhaps I
have tried too hard to be someone else without realizing at
first what I presently am. I do not know. I am not sure.
But I do know that I cannot follow this man into a house
that is so much like the one I have left this morning and
go down into the sexual embrace of a woman who might
well be my mother. And I do not know what she, my
mother, may be like in the years to come when she is
deprived of the lightning movement of my father's body
and the hammered pounding of his heart. For I do not
know when he may die. And I do not know in what
darkness she may then cry out his name nor to whom. I
do not know very much of anything, it seems, except that
I have been wrong and dishonest with others and myself.
And perhaps this man has left footprints on a soul I did
not even know that I possessed.

It is dark now on the outskirts of Springhill when the
car's headlights pick me up in their advancing beams. It
pulls over to the side and I get into its back seat. I have
trouble closing the door behind me because there is no
handle so I pull on the crank that is used for the window.
I am afraid that even it may come off in my hand. There
are two men in the front seat and I can see only the
outlines of the backs of their heads and I cannot tell very
much about them. The man in the back seat beside me is
not awfully visible either. He is tall and lean but from
what I see of his face it is difficult to tell whether he is
thirty or fifty. There are two sacks of miner's gear on the
floor at his feet and I put my sack there too because there
isn't any other place.

"Where are you from?" he asks as the car moves forward. "From Cape Breton," I say and tell him the name of
my home.

"We are too," he says, "but we're from the Island's
other side. I guess the mines are pretty well finished where

you're from. They're the old ones. They're playing out where we're from too. Where are you going now?"

"I don't know," I say, "I don't know."

"We're going to Blind River," he says. "If it doesn't work there we hear they've found uranium in Colorado and are getting ready to start sinking shafts. We might try that, but this is an old car and we don't think it'll make it to Colorado. You're welcome to come along with us though if you want. We'll carry you for a while."

"I don't know," I say, "I don't know. I'll have to think about it. I'll have to make up my mind."

The car moves forward into the night. Its headlights seek out and follow the beckoning white line which seems to lift and draw us forward, upward and inward, forever into the vastness of the dark.

"I guess your people have been on the coal over there for a long time?" asks the voice beside me.

"Yes," I say, "since 1873."

"Son of a bitch," he says, after a pause, "it seems to bust your balls and it's bound to break your heart."

THREE

The Lost Salt Gift of Blood

N OW IN the early evening the sun is flashing everything in gold. It bathes the blunt grey rocks that loom yearningly out toward Europe and it touches upon the stunted spruce and the low-lying lichens and the delicate hardy ferns and the ganglia-rooted moss and the tiny tough rock cranberries. The grey and slanting rain squalls have swept in from the sea and then departed with all the suddenness of surprise marauders. Everything before them and beneath them has been rapidly, briefly, and thoroughly drenched and now the clear droplets catch and hold the sun's infusion in a myriad of rainbow colours. Far beyond the harbour's mouth more tiny squalls seem to be forming, moving rapidly across the surface of the sea out there beyond land's end where the blue ocean turns to grey in rain and distance and the strain of eyes. Even farther out, somewhere beyond Cape Spear lies Dublin and the Irish coast; far away but still the nearest land and closer now than is Toronto or Detroit to say nothing of North America's more western cities; seeming almost hazily visible now in imagination's mist.

Overhead the ivory white gulls wheel and cry, flashing also in the purity of the sun and the clean, freshly washed air. Sometimes they glide to the blue-green surface of the harbour, squawking and garbling; at times almost standing on their pink webbed feet as if they would walk on water, flapping their wings pompously against their breasts like over-conditioned he-men who have successfully passed their body-building courses. At other times they gather in lazy groups on the rocks above the harbour's entrance murmuring softly to themselves or looking also quietly out toward what must be Ireland and the vastness of the sea.

The harbour itself is very small and softly curving, seeming like a tiny, peaceful womb nurturing the life that now lies within it but which originated from without; came from without and through the narrow, rock-tight channel that admits the entering and withdrawing sea. That sea is entering again now, forcing itself gently but inevitably through the tightness of the opening and laving the rocky walls and rising and rolling into the harbour's inner cove. The dories rise at their moorings and the tide laps higher on the piles and advances upward toward the high-water marks upon the land; the running moon-drawn tides of spring.

Around the edges of the harbour brightly coloured houses dot the wet and glistening rocks. In some ways they seem almost like defiantly optimistic horseshoe nails: yellow and scarlet and green and pink; buoyantly yet firmly permanent in the grey unsundered rock.

At the harbour's entrance the small boys are jigging for the beautifully speckled salmon-pink sea trout. Barefootedly they stand on the tide-wet rocks flicking their wrists and sending their glistening lines in shimmering golden arcs out into the rising tide. Their voices mount excitedly as they shout to one another encouragement, advice, consolation. The trout fleck dazzlingly on their sides as they are drawn toward the rocks, turning to seeming silver as they flash within the sea.

It is all of this that I see now, standing at the final road's end of my twenty-five-hundred-mile journey. The road ends here – quite literally ends at the door of a now abandoned fishing shanty some six brief yards in front of where I stand. The shanty is grey and weatherbeaten with two boarded-up windows, vanishing wind-whipped shingles and a heavy rusted padlock chained fast to a twisted door. Piled before the twisted door and its equally twisted frame are some marker buoys, a small pile of rotted rope, a broken oar and an old and rust-flaked anchor.

The option of driving my small rented Volkswagen the remaining six yards and then negotiating a tight many-twists-of-the-steering-wheel turn still exists. I would be then facing toward the west and could simply retrace the manner of my coming. I could easily drive away before anything might begin.

Instead I walk beyond the road's end and the fishing shanty and begin to descend the rocky path that winds tortuously and narrowly along and down the cliff's edge to the sea. The small stones roll and turn and scrape beside and beneath my shoes and after only a few steps the leather is nicked and scratched. My toes press hard against its straining surface.

As I approach the actual water's edge four small boys are jumping excitedly upon the glistening rocks. One of them has made a strike and is attempting to reel in his silver-turning prize. The other three have laid down their rods in their enthusiasm and are shouting encouragement and giving almost physical moral support: "Don't let him get away, John," they say. "Keep the line steady." "Hold the end of the rod up." "Reel in the slack." "Good." "What a dandy!"

Across the harbour's clear water another six or seven shout the same delirious messages. The silver-turning fish is drawn toward the rock. In the shallows he flips and arcs, his flashing body breaking the water's surface as he walks upon his tail. The small fisherman has now his rod almost completely vertical. Its tip sings and vibrates high above his head while at his feet the trout spins and curves. Both of his hands are clenched around the rod and his knuckles strain white through the water-roughened redness of small-boy hands. He does not know whether he should relinquish the rod and grasp at the lurching trout or merely heave the rod backward and flip the fish behind him. Suddenly he decides upon the latter but even as he heaves his bare feet slide out from beneath him on the smooth wetness of the rock and he slips down into the water. With a pirouetting leap the trout turns glisteningly and tears itself free. In a darting flash of darkened greenness it rights itself within the regained water and is gone. "Oh damn!" says the small fisherman, struggling upright onto his rock. He bites his lower lip to hold back the tears welling within his eyes. There is a small trickle of blood coursing down from a tiny scratch on the inside of his wrist and he is wet up to his knees. I reach down to retrieve the rod and return it to him.

Suddenly a shout rises from the opposite shore. Another line zings tautly through the water throwing off fine showers of iridescent droplets. The shouts and contagious excitement spread anew. "Don't let him get away!" "Good for you." "Hang on!" "Hang on!"

I am caught up in it myself and wish also to shout some enthusiastic advice but I do not know what to say. The trout curves up from the water in a wriggling arch and lands behind the boys in the moss and lichen that grow down to the sea-washed rocks. They race to free it from the line and proclaim about its size.

On our side of the harbour the boys begin to talk. "Where do you live?" they ask and is it far away and is it bigger than St. John's? Awkwardly I try to tell them the nature of the North American midwest. In turn I ask them if they go to school. "Yes," they say. Some of them go to St. Bonaventure's which is the Catholic school and others go to Twilling Memorial. They are all in either grade four or grade five. All of them say that they like school and that they like their teachers.

The fishing is good they say and they come here almost every evening. "Yesterday I caught me a nine-pounder," says John. Eagerly they show me all of their simple equipment. The rods are of all varieties as are the lines. At the lines' ends the leaders are thin transparencies terminating in grotesque three-clustered hooks. A foot or so from each hook there is a silver spike knotted into the leader. Some of the boys say the trout are attracted by the flashing of the spike; others say that it acts only as a weight or sinker. No line is without one.

"Here, sir," says John, "have a go. Don't get your shoes wet." Standing on the slippery rocks in my smooth-soled shoes I twice attempt awkward casts. Both times the line loops up too high and the spike splashes down far short of the running, rising life of the channel.

"Just a flick of the wrist, sir," he says, "just a flick of the wrist. You'll soon get the hang of it." His hair is red and curly and his face is splashed with freckles and his eyes are clear and blue. I attempt three or four more casts and then pass the rod back to the hands where it belongs.

And now it is time for supper. The calls float down from the women standing in the doorways of the multi-coloured houses and obediently the small fishermen gather up their equipment and their catches and prepare to ascend the narrow upward-winding paths. The sun has descended deeper into the sea and the evening has become quite cool. I recognize this with surprise and a slight shiver. In spite of the advice given to me and my own precautions my feet are wet and chilled within my shoes. No place to be unless barefooted or in rubber boots. Perhaps for me no place at all.

As we lean into the steepness of the path my young companions continue to talk, their accents broad and Irish. One of them used to have a tame sea gull at his house, had it for seven years. His older brother found it on the rocks and brought it home. His grandfather called it Joey. "Because it talked so much," explains John. It died last week and they held a funeral about a mile away from the shore where there was enough soil to dig a grave. Along the shore itself it is almost solid rock and there is no ground for a grave. It's the same with people they say. All week they have been hopefully looking along the base of the cliffs for another sea gull but have not found one. You cannot kill a sea gull they say, the government protects them because they are scavengers and keep the harbours clean.

The path is narrow and we walk in single file. By the time we reach the shanty and my rented car I am wheezing and badly out of breath. So badly out of shape for a man of thirty-three; sauna baths do nothing for your wind. The boys walk easily, laughing and talking beside me. With polite enthusiasm they comment upon my car. Again there exists the possibility of restarting the car's engine and driving back the road that I have come. After all, I have not seen a single adult except for the women calling down the news of supper. I stand and fiddle with my keys.

The appearance of the man and the dog is sudden and unexpected. We have been so casual and unaware in front of the small automobile that we have neither seen nor heard their approach along the rock-worn road. The dog is short, stocky and black and white. White hair floats and feathers freely from his sturdy legs and paws as he trots along the rock looking expectantly out into the harbour. He takes no notice of me. The man is short and stocky as well and he also appears as black and white. His rubber boots are black and his dark heavy worsted trousers are supported by a broadly scarred and blackened belt. The buckle is shaped like a dory with a fisherman standing in the bow. Above the belt there is a dark navy woollen jersey and upon his head a toque of the same material. His hair beneath the toque is white as is the three-or-four-day stubble on his face. His eyes are blue and his hands heavy, gnarled, and misshapen. It is hard to tell from looking at him whether he is in his sixties, seventies, or eighties.

"Well, it is a nice evening tonight," he says, looking first at John and then to me. "The barometer has not dropped so perhaps fair weather will continue for a day or two. It will be good for the fishing."

He picks a piece of gnarled grey driftwood from the roadside and swings it slowly back and forth in his right hand. With desperate anticipation the dog dances back and forth before him, his intense eyes glittering at the stick. When it is thrown into the harbour he barks joyously and disappears, hurling himself down the bank in a scrambling avalanche of small stones. In seconds he reappears with only his head visible, cutting a silent but rapidly advancing *V* through the quiet serenity of the harbour. The boys run to the bank's edge and shout encouragement to him – much as they had been doing earlier for one another. "It's farther out," they cry, "to the right, to the right." Almost totally submerged, he cannot see the stick he swims to find. The boys toss stones in its general direction and he raises himself out of the water to see their landing splashdowns and to change his widewaked course.

"How have you been?" asks the old man, reaching for a pipe and a pouch of tobacco and then without waiting for an answer, "perhaps you'll stay for supper. There are just the three of us now."

We begin to walk along the road in the direction that he has come. Before long the boys rejoin us accompanied by the dripping dog with the recovered stick. He waits for the old man to take it from him and then showers us all with a spray of water from his shaggy coat. The man pats and scratches the damp head and the dripping ears. He keeps the returned stick and thwacks it against his rubber boots as we continue to walk along the rocky road I have so recently travelled in my Volkswagen.

Within a few yards the houses begin to appear upon our left. Frame and flat-roofed, they cling to the rocks looking down into the harbour. In storms their windows are splashed by the sea but now their bright colours are buoyantly brave in the shadows of the descending dusk. At the third gate, John, the man, and the dog turn in. I follow them. The remaining boys continue on; they wave and say, "So long."

The path that leads through the narrow whitewashed gate has had its stone worn smooth by the passing of countless feet. On either side there is a row of small, smooth stones, also neatly whitewashed, and seeming like a procession of large white eggs or tiny unbaked loaves of bread. Beyond these stones and also on either side, there are some cast-off tires also whitewashed and serving as flower beds. Within each whitened circumference the colourful low-lying flowers nod; some hardy strain of pansies or perhaps marigolds. The path leads on to the square green house, with its white borders and shutters. On one side of the wooden doorstep a skate blade has been nailed, for the wiping off of feet, and beyond the swinging screen door there is a porch which smells saltily of the sea. A variety of sou'westers and rubber boots and mitts and caps hang from the driven nails or lie at the base of the wooden walls.

Beyond the porch there is the kitchen where the woman is at work. All of us enter. The dog walks across the linoleum-covered floor, his nails clacking, and flings himself with a contented sigh beneath the wooden table. Almost instantly he is asleep, his coat still wet from his swim within the sea.

The kitchen is small. It has an iron cookstove, a table against one wall and three or four handmade chairs of wood. There is also a wooden rocking-chair covered by a cushion. The rockers are so thin from years of use that it is hard to believe they still function. Close by the table there is a wash-stand with two pails of water upon it. A wash-basin hangs from a driven nail in its side and above it is an old-fashioned mirrored medicine cabinet. There is also a large cupboard, a low-lying couch, and a window facing upon the sea. On the walls a barometer hangs as well as two pictures, one of a rather jaunty young couple taken many years ago. It is yellowed and rather indistinct; the woman in a long dress with her hair done up in ringlets, the man in a serge suit that is slightly too large for him and with a tweed cap pulled rakishly over his right eye. He has an accordion strapped over his shoulders and his hands are fanned out on the buttons and keys. The other picture is of the Christ-child. Beneath it is written, "Sweet Heart of Jesus Pray for Us."

The woman at the stove is tall and fine featured. Her grey hair is combed briskly back from her forehead and neatly coiled with a large pin at the base of her neck. Her eyes are as grey as the storm scud of the sea. Her age, like her husband's, is difficult to guess. She wears a blue print dress, a plain blue apron and low-heeled brown shoes. She is turning fish within a frying pan when we enter.

Her eyes contain only mild surprise as she first regards me. Then with recognition they glow in open hostility which in turn subsides and yields to self-control. She continues at the stove while the rest of us sit upon the chairs.

During the meal that follows we are reserved and shy in our lonely adult ways; groping for and protecting what perhaps may be the only awful dignity we possess. John, unheedingly, talks on and on. He is in the fifth grade and is doing well. They are learning percentages and the mysteries of decimals; to change a percent to a decimal fraction you move the decimal point two places to the left and drop the percent sign. You always, always do so. They are learning the different breeds of domestic animals: the four main breeds of dairy cattle are Holstein, Ayrshire, Guernsey, and Jersey. He can play the mouth organ and will demonstrate after supper. He has twelve lobster traps of his own. They were originally broken ones thrown up on the rocky shore by storms. Ira, he says nodding toward the old man, helped him fix them, nailing on new lathes and knitting new headings. Now they are set along the rocks near the harbour's entrance. He is averaging a pound a trap and the "big" fishermen say that that is better than some of them are doing. He is saving his money in a little imitation keg that was also washed up on the shore. He would like to buy an outboard motor for the small reconditioned skiff he now uses to visit his traps. At present he has only oars.

"John here has the makings of a good fisherman," says the old man. "He's up at five most every morning when I am putting on the fire. He and the dog are already out along the shore and back before I've made tea."

"When I was in Toronto," says John, "no one was ever up before seven. I would make my own tea and wait. It was wonderful sad. There were gulls there though, flying over Toronto harbour. We went to see them on two Sundays."

After the supper we move the chairs back from the table. The woman clears away the dishes and the old man turns on the radio. First he listens to the weather forecast and then turns to short wave where he picks up the conversations from the offshore fishing boats. They are conversations of catches and winds and tides and of the women left behind on the rocky shores. John appears with his mouth organ, standing at a respectful distance. The old man notices him, nods, and shuts off the radio. Rising, he goes upstairs, the sound of his feet echoing down to us. Returning he carries an old and battered accordion. "My fingers have so much rheumatism," he says, "that I find it hard to play anymore."

Seated, he slips his arms through the straps and begins the squeezing accordion motions. His wife takes off her apron and stands behind him with one hand upon his shoulder. For a moment they take on the essence of the once young people in the photograph. They begin to sing:

Come all ye fair and tender ladies
Take warning how you court your men
They're like the stars on a summer's morning
First they'll appear and then they're gone.

I wish I were a tiny sparrow
And I had wings and I could fly
I'd fly away to my own true lover
And all he'd ask I would deny.

Alas I'm not a tiny sparrow
I have not wings nor can fly

And on this earth in grief and sorrow
I am bound until I die.

John sits on one of the home-made chairs playing his mouth organ. He seems as all mouth-organ players the world over: his right foot tapping out the measures and his small shoulders now round and hunched above the cupped hand instrument.

"Come now and sing with us, John," says the old man.

Obediently he takes the mouth organ from his mouth and shakes the moisture drops upon his sleeve. All three of them begin to sing, spanning easily the half century of time that touches their extremes. The old and the young singing now their songs of loss in different comprehensions. Stranded here, alien of my middle generation, I tap my leather foot self-consciously upon the linoleum. The words sweep up and swirl about my head. Fog does not touch like snow yet it is more heavy and more dense. Oh moisture comes in many forms!

All alone as I strayed by the banks of the river
Watching the moonbeams at evening of day
All alone as I wandered I spied a young stranger
Weeping and wailing with many a sigh.

Weeping for one who is now lying lonely
Weeping for one who no mortal can save
As the foaming dark waters flow silently past him
Onward they flow over young Jenny's grave.

Oh Jenny my darling come tarry here with me
Don't leave me alone, love, distracted in pain
For as death is the dagger that plied us usunder
Wide is the gulf, love, between you and I.

After the singing stops we all sit rather uncomfortably for a moment. The mood seeming to hang heavily upon our shoulders. Then with my single exception all come suddenly to action. John gets up and takes his battered school books to the kitchen table. The dog jumps up on a chair beside him and watches solemnly in a supervisory manner. The woman takes some navy yarn the colour of her husband's jersey and begins to knit. She is making another jersey and is working on the sleeve. The old man rises and beckons me to follow him into the tiny parlour. The stuffed furniture is old and worn. There is a tiny wood-burning heater in the centre of the room. It stands on a square of galvanized metal which protects the floor from falling, burning coals. The stovepipe rises and vanishes into the wall on its way to the upstairs. There is an old-fashioned mantelpiece on the wall behind the stove. It is covered with odd shapes of driftwood from the shore and a variety of exotically shaped bottles, blue and green and red, which are from the shore as well. There are pictures here too: of the couple in the other picture; and one of them with their five daughters; and one of the five daughters by themselves. In that far-off picture time all of the daughters seem roughly between the ages of ten and eighteen. The youngest has the reddest hair of all. So red that it seems to triumph over the non-photographic colours of lonely black and white. The pictures are in standard wooden frames.

From behind the ancient chesterfield the old man pulls a collapsible card table and pulls down its warped and shaky legs. Also from behind the chesterfield he takes a faded checkerboard and a large old-fashioned matchbox of rattling wooden checkers. The spine of the board is almost cracked through and is strengthened by layers of adhesive tape. The checkers are circumferences of wood sawed from a length of broom handle. They are about three quarters of an inch thick. Half of them are painted a very bright blue and the other half an equally eye-catching red. "John made these," says the old man, "all of them are not really the same thickness but they are good enough. He gave it a good try."

We begin to play checkers. He takes the blue and I the red. The house is silent with only the click-clack of the knitting needles sounding through the quiet rooms. From time to time the old man lights his pipe, digging out the old ashes with a flattened nail and tamping in the fresh tobacco with the same nail's head. The blue smoke winds lazily and haphazardly toward the low-beamed ceiling. The game is solemn as is the next and then the next. Neither of us loses all of the time.

"It is time for some of us to be in bed," says the old woman after a while. She gathers up her knitting and rises from her chair. In the kitchen John neatly stacks his school books on one corner of the table in anticipation of the morning. He goes outside for a moment and then returns. Saying good-night very formally he goes up the stairs to bed. In a short while the old woman follows, her footsteps travelling the same route.

We continue to play our checkers, wreathed in smoke and only partially aware of the muffled footfalls sounding softly above our heads.

When the old man gets up to go outside I am not really surprised, any more than I am when he returns with the brown, ostensible vinegar jug. Poking at the declining kitchen fire, he moves the kettle about seeking the warmest spot on the cooling stove. He takes two glasses from the cupboard, a sugar bowl and two spoons. The kettle begins to boil.

Even before tasting it, I know the rum to be strong and overproof. It comes at night and in fog from the French islands of St. Pierre and Miquelon. Coming over in the low-throttled fishing boats, riding in imitation gas cans. He mixes the rum and the sugar first, watching them marry and dissolve. Then to prevent the breakage of the glasses he places a teaspoon in each and adds the boiling water. The odour rises richly, its sweetness hung in steam. He brings the glasses to the table, holding them by their tops so that his fingers will not burn.

We do not say anything for some time, sitting upon the chairs, while the sweetened, heated richness moves warmly through and from our stomachs and spreads upward to our brains. Outside the wind begins to blow, moaning and faintly rattling the window's whitened shutters. He rises and brings refills. We are warm within the dark and still within the wind. A clock strikes regularly the strokes of ten.

It is difficult to talk at times with or without liquor; difficult to achieve the actual act of saying. Sitting still we listen further to the rattle of the wind; not knowing where nor how we should begin. Again the glasses are refilled.

"When she married in Toronto," he says at last, "we figured that maybe John should be with her and with her husband. That maybe he would be having more of a chance there in the city. But we would be putting it off and it weren't until nigh on two years ago that he went. Went with a woman from down the cove going to visit her daughter. Well, what was wrong was that we missed him wonderful awful. More fearful than we ever thought. Even the dog. Just pacing the floor and looking out the window and walking along the rocks of the shore. Like us had no moorings, lost in the fog or on the ice-floes in a snow squall. Nigh sick unto our hearts we was. Even the grandmother who before that was maybe thinking small to herself that he was trouble in her old age. Ourselves having never had no sons only daughters."

He pauses, then rising goes upstairs and returns with an envelope. From it he takes a picture which shows two young people standing self-consciously before a half-ton pickup with a wooden extension ladder fastened to its side. They appear to be in their middle twenties. The door of the truck has the information: "Jim Farrell, Toronto: Housepainting, Eavestroughing, Aluminum Siding, Phone 535-3484," lettered on its surface.

"This was in the last letter," he says. "That Farrell I guess was a nice enough fellow, from Heartsick Bay he was.

"Anyway they could have no more peace with John than we could without him. Like I says he was here too long before his going and it all took ahold of us the way it will. They sent word that he was coming on the plane to

St. John's with a woman they'd met through a Newfoundland club. I was to go to St. John's to meet him. Well, it
was all wrong the night before the going. The signs all bad;
the grandmother knocked off the lampshade and it broke
in a hunnerd pieces – the sign of death; and the window
blind fell and clattered there on the floor and then lied
still. And the dog runned around like he was crazy,
moanen and cryen worse than the swiles does out on the
ice, and throwen hisself against the walls and jumpen on
the table and at the window where the blind fell until we
would have to be letten him out. But it be no better for he
runned and throwed hisself in the sea and then come back
and howled outside the same window and jumped against
the wall, splashen the water from his coat all over it. Then
he be runnen back to the sea again. All the neighbours
heard him and said I should bide at home and not go to
St. John's at all. We be all wonderful scared and not know
what to do and the next mornen, first thing I drops me
knife.

"But still I feels I has to go. It be foggy all the day and
everyone be thinken the plane won't come or be able to
land. And I says, small to myself, now here in the fog be
the bad luck and the death but then there the plane be,
almost like a ghost ship comen out the fog with all its
lights shinen. I think maybe he won't be on it but soon he
comen through the fog, first with the woman and then
see'n me and starten to run, closer and closer till I can feel
him in me arms and the tears on both our cheeks. Powerful strange how things will take one. That night they be
killed."

From the envelope that contained the picture he draws
forth a tattered clipping:

Jennifer Farrell of Roncesvalles Avenue was instantly
killed early this morning and her husband James died later
in emergency at St. Joseph's Hospital. The accident occurred
about 2 A.M. when the pickup truck in which they were
travelling went out of control on Queen St. W. and struck a

utility pole. It is thought that bad visibility caused by a heavy fog may have contributed to the accident. The Farrells were originally from Newfoundland.

Again he moves to refill the glasses. "We be all alone," he says. "All our other daughters married and far away in Montreal, Toronto, or the States. Hard for them to come back here, even to visit; they comes only every three years or so for perhaps a week. So we be hav'n only him."

And now my head begins to reel even as I move to the filling of my own glass. Not waiting this time for the courtesy of his offer. Making myself perhaps too much at home with this man's glass and this man's rum and this man's house and all the feelings of his love. Even as I did before. Still locked again for words.

Outside we stand and urinate, turning our backs to the seeming gale so as not to splash our wind-snapped trousers. We are almost driven forward to rock upon our toes and settle on our heels, so blow the gusts. Yet in spite of all, the stars shine clearly down. It will indeed be a good day for the fishing and this wind eventually will calm. The salt hangs heavy in the air and the water booms against the rugged rocks. I take a stone and throw it against the wind into the sea.

Going up the stairs we clutch the wooden bannister unsteadily and say good-night.

The room has changed very little. The window rattles in the wind and the unfinished beams sway and creak. The room is full of sound. Like a foolish Lockwood I approach the window although I hear no voice. There is no Catherine who cries to be let in. Standing unsteadily on one foot when required I manage to undress, draping my trousers across the wooden chair. The bed is clean. It makes no sound. It is plain and wooden, its mattress stuffed with hay or kelp. I feel it with my hand and pull back the heavy patchwork quilts. Still I do not go into it. Instead I go back to the door which has no knob but only an ingenious latch formed from a twisted nail. Turning it, I go out into the hallway. All is dark and the house seems even more inclined to creak where there is no window. Feeling along the wall with my outstretched hand I find the door quite easily. It is closed with the same kind of latch and not difficult to open. But no one waits on the other side. I stand and bend my ear to hear the even sound of my one son's sleeping. He does not beckon any more than the nonexistent voice in the outside wind. I hesitate to touch the latch for fear that I may waken him and disturb his dreams. And if I did what would I say? Yet I would like to see him in his sleep this once and see the room with the quiet bed once more and the wooden chair beside it from off an old wrecked trawler. There is no boiled egg or shaker of salt or glass of water waiting on the chair within this closed room's darkness.

Once though there was a belief held in the outports, that if a girl would see her own true lover she should boil an egg and scoop out half the shell and fill it with salt. Then she should take it to bed with her and eat it, leaving a glass of water by her bedside. In the night her future husband or a vision of him would appear and offer her the glass. But she must only do it once.

It is the type of belief that bright young graduate students were collecting eleven years ago for the theses and archives of North America and also, they hoped, for their own fame. Even as they sought the near-Elizabethan songs and ballads that had sailed from County Kerry and from Devon and Cornwall. All about the wild, wide sea and the flashing silver dagger and the lost and faithless lover. Echoes to and from the lovely, lonely hills and glens of West Virginia and the standing stones of Tennessee.

Across the hall the old people are asleep. The old man's snoring rattles as do the windows; except that now and then there are catching gasps within his breath. In three or four short hours he will be awake and will go down to light his fire. I turn and walk back softly to my room.

Within the bed the warm sweetness of the rum is heavy and intense. The darkness presses down upon me but still it brings no sleep. There are no voices and no shadows that are real. There are only walls of memory touched restlessly by flickers of imagination.

Oh I would like to see my way more clearly. I, who have never understood the mystery of fog. I would perhaps like to capture it in a jar like the beautiful childhood butterflies that always die in spite of the airholes punched with nails in the covers of their captivity – leaving behind the vapours of their lives and deaths; or perhaps as the unknowing child who collects the grey moist condoms from the lovers' lanes only to have them taken from him and to be told to wash his hands. Oh I have collected many things I did not understand.

And perhaps now I should go and say, oh son of my *summa cum laude* loins, come away from the lonely gulls and the silver trout and I will take you to the land of the Tastee Freeze where you may sleep till ten of nine. And I will show you the elevator to the apartment on the sixteenth floor and introduce you to the buzzer system and the yards of the wrought-iron fences where the Doberman pinscher runs silently at night. Or may I offer you the money that is the fruit of my collecting and my most successful life? Or shall I wait to meet you in some known or unknown bitterness like Yeats's Cuchulain by the wind-whipped sea or as Sohrab and Rustum by the future flowing river?

Again I collect dreams. For I do not know enough of the fog on Toronto's Queen St. West and the grinding crash of the pickup and of lost and misplaced love.

I am up early in the morning as the man kindles the fire from the driftwood splinters. The outside light is breaking and the wind is calm. John tumbles down the stairs. Scarcely stopping to splash his face and pull on his jacket, he is gone, accompanied by the dog. The old man smokes his pipe and waits for the water to boil. When it does he pours some into the teapot then passes the kettle to me. I take it to the wash-stand and fill the small tin basin in readiness for my shaving. My face looks back from the mirrored cabinet. The woman softly descends the stairs.

"I think I will go back today," I say while looking into

the mirror at my face and at those in the room behind me. I try to emphasize the "I." "I just thought I would like to make this trip – again. I think I can leave the car in St. John's and fly back directly." The woman begins to move about the table, setting out the round white plates. The man quietly tamps his pipe.

The door opens and John and the dog return. They have been down along the shore to see what has happened throughout the night. "Well, John," says the old man, "what did you find?"

He opens his hand to reveal a smooth round stone. It is of the deepest green inlaid with veins of darkest ebony. It has been worn and polished by the unrelenting restlessness of the sea and buffed and burnished by the gravelled sand. All of its inadequacies have been removed and it glows with the lustre of near perfection.

"It is very beautiful," I say.

"Yes," he says, "I like to collect them." Suddenly he looks up to my eyes and thrusts the stone toward me. "Here," he says, "would you like to have it?"

Even as I reach out my hand I turn my head to the others in the room. They are both looking out through the window to the sea.

"Why, thank you," I say. "Thank you very much. Yes, I would. Thank you. Thanks." I take it from his outstretched hand and place it in my pocket.

We eat our breakfast in near silence. After it is finished the boy and dog go out once more. I prepare to leave.

"Well, I must go," I say, hesitating at the door. "It will take me a while to get to St. John's." I offer my hand to the man. He takes it in his strong fingers and shakes it firmly.

"Thank you," says the woman. "I don't know if you know what I mean but thank you."

"I think I do," I say. I stand and fiddle with the keys. "I would somehow like to help or keep in touch but . . . "

"But there is no phone," he says, "and both of us can hardly write. Perhaps that's why we never told you. John is getting to be a pretty good hand at it though."

"Good-bye," we say again, "good-bye, good-bye."

The sun is shining clearly now and the small boats are putt-putting about the harbour. I enter my unlocked car and start its engine. The gravel turns beneath the wheels. I pass the house and wave to the man and woman standing in the yard.

On a distant cliff the children are shouting. Their voices carol down through the sun-washed air and the dogs are curving and dancing about them in excited circles. They are carrying something that looks like a crippled gull. Perhaps they will make it well. I toot the horn. "Good-bye," they shout and wave, "good-bye, good-bye."

The airport terminal is strangely familiar. A symbol of impermanence, it is itself glisteningly permanent. Its formica surfaces have been designed to stay. At the counter a middle-aged man in mock exasperation is explaining to the girl that it is Newark he wishes to go to, *not* New York.

There are not many of us and soon we are ticketed and lifting through and above the sun-shot fog. The meals are served in tinfoil and in plastic. We eat above the clouds looking at the tips of wings.

The man beside me is a heavy-equipment salesman who has been trying to make a sale to the developers of Labrador's resources. He has been away a week and is returning to his wife and children.

Later in the day we land in the middle of the continent. Because of the changing time zones the distance we have come seems eerily unreal. The heat shimmers in little waves upon the runway. This is the equipment salesman's final destination while for me it is but the place where I must change flights to continue even farther into the heartland. Still we go down the wheeled-up stairs together, donning our sunglasses, and stepping across the heated concrete and through the terminal's electronic doors. The salesman's wife stands waiting along with two small children who are the first to see him. They race toward him with their arms outstretched. "Daddy, Daddy," they cry, "what did you bring me? What did you bring me?"

FOUR

The Return

IT IS an evening during the summer that I am ten years old and I am on a train with my parents as it rushes toward the end of eastern Nova Scotia. "You'll be able to see it any minute now, Alex," says my father excitedly, "look out the window, any minute now."

He is standing in the aisle by this time with his left hand against the overhead baggage rack while leaning over me and over my mother who is in the seat by the window. He has grasped my right hand in his right and when I look up it is first into the whiteness of his shirt front arching over me and then into the fine features of his face, the blueness of his eyes and his wavy reddish hair. He is very tall and athletic looking. He is forty-five.

"Oh Angus, sit down," says my mother with mingled patience and exasperation, "he'll see it soon enough. We're almost there. Please sit down; people are looking at you."

My left hand lies beside my mother's right on the green upholstered cushion. My mother has brown eyes and brown hair and is three years younger than my father. She is very beautiful and her picture is often in the society pages of the papers in Montreal which is where we live.

"There it is," shouts my father triumphantly. "Look Alex, there's Cape Breton!" He takes his left hand down from the baggage rack and points across us to the blueness that is the Strait of Canso, with the gulls hanging almost stationary above the tiny fishing boats and the dark green of the spruce and fir mountains rising out of the water and trailing white wisps of mist about them like discarded ribbons hanging about a newly opened package.

The train lurches and he almost loses his balance and quickly has to replace his hand on the baggage rack. He is squeezing my right hand so hard he is hurting me and I can feel my fingers going numb within his grip. I would like to mention it but I do not know how to do so politely and I know he does not mean to cause me pain.

"Yes, there it is," says my mother without much enthusiasm, "now you can sit down like everybody else."

He does so but continues to hold my hand very fiercely. "Here," says my mother not unkindly, and passes him a Kleenex over my head. He takes it quietly and I am reminded of the violin records which he has at home in Montreal. My mother does not like them and says they all sound the same so he only plays them when she is out and we are alone. Then it is a time like church, very solemn and serious and sad and I am not supposed to talk but I do not know what else I am supposed to do; especially when my father cries.

Now the train is getting ready to go across the water on a boat. My father releases my hand and starts gathering our luggage because we are to change trains on the other side. After this is done we all go out on the deck of the ferry and watch the Strait as we groan over its placid surface and churn its tranquillity into the roiling turmoil of our own white-watered wake.

My father goes back into the train and reappears with the cheese sandwich which I did not eat and then we go to the stern of the ferry where the other people are tossing food to the convoy of screaming gulls which follows us on our way. The gulls are the whitest things that I have ever seen; whiter than the sheets on my bed at home, or the pink-eyed rabbit that died, or the winter's first snow. I think that since they are so beautiful they should some-how have more manners and in some way be more refined. There is one mottled brown, who feels very ill at ease and flies low and to the left of the noisy main flock. When he ventures into the thick of the fray his fellows scream and peck at him and drive him away. All three of us try to toss our pieces of cheese sandwich to him or into the water directly before him. He is so lonesome and all alone.

When we get to the other side we change trains. A blond young man is hanging from a slowly chugging train with one hand and drinking from a bottle which he holds in the other. I think it is a very fine idea and ask my father to buy me some pop. He says he will later but is strangely embarrassed. As we cross the tracks to our train, the blond young man begins to sing: "There once was an Indian maid." It is not the nice version but the dirty one which I and my friends have learned from the bigger boys in the sixth grade. I have somehow never before thought of grown-ups singing it. My parents are now walking very fast, practically dragging me by the hand over the troublesome tracks. They are both very red-faced and we all pretend we do not hear the voice that is receding in the distance.

When we are seated on the new train I see that my mother is very angry. "Ten years," she snaps at my father, "ten years I've raised this child in the city of Montreal and he has never seen an adult drink liquor out of a bottle, nor heard that kind of language. We have not been here five minutes and that is the first thing he sees and hears." She is on the verge of tears.

"Take it easy, Mary," says my father soothingly. "He doesn't understand. It's all right."

"It's not all right," says my mother passionately. "It's not all right at all. It's dirty and filthy and I must have been out of my mind to agree to this trip. I wish we were going back tomorrow."

The train starts to move and before long we are rattling along the shore. There are fishermen in little boats who wave good-naturedly at the train and I wave back. Later there are the black gashes of coal mines which look like scabs upon the greenness of the hills and the blueness of the ocean and I wonder if these are the mines in which my relatives work.

This train goes much slower than the last one and seems to stop every five minutes. Some of the people around us are talking in a language that I know is Gaelic although I do not understand it, others are sprawled out in their seats, some of them drowsing with their feet stuck out in the aisle. At the far end of the aisle two empty bottles roll endlessly back and forth clinking against themselves and the steel-bottomed seats. The coach creaks and sways.

The station is small and brown. There is a wooden platform in front of it illuminated by lights which shine down from two tall poles and are bombarded by squads of suicidal moths and June bugs. Beneath the lights there are little clusters of darkly clad men who talk and chew tobacco, and some ragged boys about my own age who lean against battered bicycles waiting for the bundles of newspapers that thud on the platform before their feet.

Two tall men detach themselves from one of the groups and approach us. I know they are both my uncles although I have only seen the younger one before. He lived at our house during part of the year that was the first grade and used to wrestle with me on the floor and play the violin records when no one was in. Then one day he was gone forever to survive only in my mother's neutral "It was the year your brother was here," or the more pointed "It was the year your drunken brother was here."

Now both men are very polite. They shake hands with my father and say "Hello Angie" and then, taking off their caps, "How do you do" to my mother. Then each of them lifts me up in the air. The younger one asks me if I remember him and I say "Yes" and he laughs, and puts me down. They carry our suitcases to a taxi and then we all bounce along a very rough street and up a hill, bump, bump, and stop before a large dark house which we enter.

In the kitchen of the house there are a great many

people sitting around a big coal-burning stove even though it is summer. They all get up when we come in and shake hands and the women put their arms around my mother. Then I am introduced to the grandparents I have never seen. My grandmother is very tall with hair almost as white as the afternoon's gulls and eyes like the sea over which they flew. She wears a long black dress with a blue checkered apron over it and lifts me off my feet in powerful hands so that I can kiss her and look into her eyes. She smells of soap and water and hot rolls and asks me how I like living in Montreal. I have never lived anywhere else so I say I guess it is all right.

My grandfather is short and stocky with heavy arms and very big hands. He has brown eyes and his once red hair is almost all white now except for his eyebrows and the hair of his nostrils. He has a white moustache which reminds me of the walrus picture at school and the bottom of it is stained brown by the tobacco that he is chewing even now and spitting the juice into a coal scuttle which he keeps beside his chair. He is wearing a blue plaid shirt and brown trousers supported by heavy suspenders. He too lifts me up although he does not kiss me and he smells of soap and water and tobacco and leather. He asks me if I saw any girls that I liked on the train. I say "No," and he laughs and lowers me to the floor.

And now it is later and the conversation has died down and the people have gradually filtered out into the night until there are just the three of us, and my grandparents, and after a while my grandmother and my mother go upstairs to finalize the sleeping arrangements. My grandfather puts rum and hot water and sugar into two glasses and gives one to my father and then allows me to sit on his lap even though I am ten, and gives me sips from his glass. He is very different from Grandpa Gilbert in Montreal who wears white shirts and dark suits with a vest and a gold watch-chain across the front.

"You have been a long time coming home," he says to my father. "If you had come through that door as often as

I've thought of you I'd've replaced the hinges a good
many times."

"I know, I've tried, I've wanted to, but it's different in
Montreal you know."

"Yes I guess so. I just never figured it would be like this.
It seems so far away and we get old so quickly and a man
always feels a certain way about his oldest son. I guess in
some ways it is a good thing that we do not all go to
school. I could never see myself being owned by my
woman's family."

"Please don't start that already," says my father a little
angrily. "I am not owned by anybody and you know it. I
am a lawyer and I am in partnership with another lawyer
who just happens to be my father-in-law. That's all."

"Yes, that's all," says my grandfather and gives me
another sip from his glass. "Well, to change the subject, is
this the only one you have after being married eleven
years?"

My father is now red-faced like he was when we heard
the young man singing. He says heatedly: "You know
you're not changing the subject at all. I know what you're
getting at. I know what you mean."

"Do you?" asks my grandfather quietly. "I thought perhaps that was different in Montreal too."

The two women come downstairs just as I am having
another sip from the glass. "Oh Angus what can you be
thinking of?" screams my mother rushing protectively
toward me.

"Mary, please!" says my father almost desperately,
"there's nothing wrong."

My grandfather gets up very rapidly, sets me on the
chair he has just vacated, drains the controversial glass,
rinses it in the sink and says, "Well, time for the working
class to be in bed. Good-night all." He goes up the stairs
walking very heavily and we can hear his boots as he
thumps them on the floor.

"I'll put him to bed, Mary," says my father nodding

toward me. "I know where he sleeps. Why don't you go to bed now? You're tired."

"Yes, all right," says my mother very gently. "I'm sorry. I didn't mean to hurt his feelings. Good-night." She kisses me and also my grandmother and her footsteps fade quietly up the stairs.

"I'm sorry Ma, she didn't mean it the way it sounded," says my father.

"I know. She finds it very different from what she's used to. And we are older and don't bounce back the way we once did. He is seventy-six now and the mine is hard on him and he feels he must work harder than ever to do his share. He works with different ones of the boys and he tells me that sometimes he thinks they are carrying him just because he is their father. He never felt that way with you or Alex but of course you were all much younger then. Still he always somehow felt that because those years between high school and college were so good that you would both come back to him some day."

"But Ma, it can't be that way. I was twenty then and Alex nineteen and he was only in his early fifties and we both wanted to go to college so we could be something else. And we paid him back the money he loaned us and he seemed to want us to go to school then."

"He did not know what it was then. Nor I. And when you gave him back the money it was as if that was not what he'd had in mind at all. And what is the something you two became? A lawyer whom we never see and a doctor who committed suicide when he was twenty-seven. Lost to us the both of you. More lost than Andrew who is buried under tons of rock two miles beneath the sea and who never saw a college door."

"Well, he should have," says my father bitterly, "so should they all instead of being exploited and burrowing beneath the sea or becoming alcoholics that cannot even do that."

"I have my alcoholic," says my grandmother now

standing very tall, "who was turned out of my Montreal lawyer's home."

"But I couldn't do anything with him, Ma, and it's different there. You just can't be that way, and – and – oh hell, I don't know; If I were by myself he could have stayed forever."

"I know," says my grandmother now very softly, putting her hand upon his shoulder, "it's not you. But it seems that we can only stay forever if we stay right here. As we have stayed to the seventh generation. Because in the end that is all there is – just staying. I have lost three children at birth but I've raised eight sons. I have one a lawyer and one a doctor who committed suicide, one who died in coal beneath the sea and one who is a drunkard and four who still work the coal like their father and those four are all that I have that stand by me. It is these four that carry their father now that he needs it, and it is these four that carry the drunkard, that dug two days for Andrew's body and that have given me thirty grandchildren in my old age."

"I know, Ma," says my father, "I know that and I appreciate it all, everything. It is just that, well somehow we just can't live in a clan system anymore. We have to see beyond ourselves and our own families. We have to live in the twentieth century."

"Twentieth century?" says my grandmother spreading her big hands across her checkered apron. "What is the twentieth century to me if I cannot have my own?"

It is morning now and I awake to the argument of the English sparrows outside my window and the fingers of the sun upon the floor. My parents are in my room discussing my clothes. "He really doesn't need them," says my father patiently. "But Angus I don't want him to look like a little savage," replies my mother as she lays out my newly pressed pants and shirt at the foot of the bed.

Downstairs I learn that my grandfather has already gone to work and as I solemnly eat my breakfast like a little old man beyond my years, I listen to the violin music on the radio and watch my grandmother as she spreads butter on the top of the baking loaves and pokes the coals of her fire with a fierce enthusiasm that sends clouds of smoke billowing up to spread themselves against the yellowed paint upon her ceiling.

Then the little boys come in and stand shyly against the wall. There are seven of them and they are all between six and ten. "These are your cousins," says my grandmother to me and to them she says, "this is Alex from Montreal. He is come to visit with us and you are to be nice to him because he is one of our own."

Then I and my cousins go outside because it is what we are supposed to do and we ask one another what grades we are in and I say I dislike my teacher and they mostly say they like theirs which is a possibility I have never considered before. And then we talk about hockey and I try to remember the times I have been to the Forum in Montreal and what I think about Richard.

And then we go down through the town which is black and smoky and has no nice streets nor flashing lights like Montreal, and when I dawdle behind I suddenly find myself confronted by two older boys who say: "Hey, where'd y'get them sissy clothes?" I do not know what I am supposed to do until my cousins come back and surround me like the covered wagons around the women and children of the cowboy shows, when the Indians attack.

"This is our cousin," say the oldest two simultaneously and I think they are very fine and brave for they too are probably a little bit ashamed of me and I wonder if I would do the same for them. I have never before thought that perhaps I have been lonely all of my short life and I wish that I had brothers of my own – even sisters perhaps.

My almost-attackers wait awhile scuffing their shoes on the ashy sidewalk and then they separate and allow us to pass like a little band of cavalry going through the mountains.

We continue down through the town and farther

beyond to the seashore where the fishermen are mending their gear and pumping the little boats in which they allow us to play. Then we skip rocks on the surface of the sea and I skip one six times and then stop because I know I have made an impression and doubt if I am capable of an encore.

And then we climb up a high, high hill that tumbles into the sea and a cousin says we will go to see the bull who apparently lives about a mile away. We are really out in the country now and it is getting hot and when I go to loosen my tie the collar button comes off and is forever lost in the grass through which we pass.

The bull lives in a big barn and my cousins ask an old man who looks like my grandfather if he expects any cows today. He says that he does not know, that you cannot tell about those things. We can look at the bull if we wish but we must not tease him nor go too close. He is very big and brown and white with a ring in his nose and he paws the floor of his stall and makes low noises while lowering his head and swinging it from side to side. Just as we are ready to leave the old man comes in carrying a long wooden staff which he snaps onto the bull's nose ring. "Well, it looks like you laddies are in luck," he says, "now be careful and get out of the way." I follow my cousins who run out into a yard where a man who has just arrived is standing holding a nervous cow by a halter and we sit appreciatively on the top rail of the wooden fence and watch the old man as he leads out the bull who is now moaning and dripping and frothing at the mouth. I have never seen anything like this before and watch with awe this something that is both beautiful and terrible and I know that I will somehow not be able to tell my mother to whom I have told almost everything important that has happened in my young life.

And later as we leave, the old man's wife gives us some apples and says, "John you should be ashamed of yourself; in front of these children. There are some things that have to be but are not for children's eyes." The chastised old man nods and looks down upon his shoes but then looks up at us very gravely from beneath his bushy eyebrows, looks at us in a very special way and I know that it is only because we are all boys that he does this and that the look as it excludes the woman simultaneously includes us in something that I know and feel but cannot understand.

We go back then to the town and it is late afternoon and we have eaten nothing but the apples and as we climb the hill toward my grandparents' house I see my father striding down upon us with his newspaper under his arm.

He is not disturbed that I have stayed away so long and seems almost to envy us our unity and our dirt as he stands so straight and lonely in the prison of his suit and inquires of our day. And so we reply as children do, that we have been "playing," which is the old inadequate message sent forth across the chasm of our intervening years to fall undelivered and unreceived into the nothingness between.

He is going down to the mine, he says, to meet the men when they come off their shift at four and he will take me if I wish. So I separate from my comrade-cousins and go back down the hill holding on to his hand which is something I do not often do. I think that I will tell him about the bull but instead I ask: "Why do all the men chew tobacco?"

"Oh," he says, "because it is a part of them and of their way of life. They do that instead of smoking."

"But why don't they smoke?"

"Because they are underground so much of their lives and they cannot light a match or a lighter or carry any open flame down there. It's because of the gas. Flame might cause an explosion and kill them all."

"But when they're not down there they could smoke cigarettes like Grandpa Gilbert in a silver cigarette holder and Mama says that chewing tobacco is a filthy habit."

"I know but these people are not at all like Grandpa

Gilbert and there are things that Mama doesn't understand. It is not that easy to change what is a part of you."

We are approaching the mine now and everything is black and grimy and the heavily laden trucks are groaning past us. "Did you used to chew tobacco?"

"Yes, a very long time ago before you were ever thought of."

"And was it hard for you to stop?"

"Yes it was, Alex," he says quietly, "more difficult than you will ever know."

We are now at the wash-house and the trains from the underground are thundering up out of the darkness and the men are jumping off and laughing and shouting to one another in a way that reminds me of recess. They are completely black with the exception of little white half-moons beneath their eyes and the eyes themselves. My grandfather is walking toward us between two of my uncles. He is not so tall as they nor does he take such long strides and they are pacing themselves to keep even with him the way my father sometimes does with me. Even his moustache is black or a very dirty grey except for the bottom of it where the tobacco stains it brown.

As they walk they are taking off their headlamps and unfastening the batteries from the broad belts which I feel would be very fine for carrying holsters and six-guns. They are also fishing for the little brass discs which bear their identification numbers. My father says that if they should be killed in the underground these little discs would tell who each man was. It does not seem like much consolation to me.

At a wicket that looks like the post office the men line up and pass their lamps and the little discs to an old man with glasses. He puts the lamps on a rack and the discs on a large board behind his back. Each disc goes on its special little numbered hook and this shows that its owner has returned. My grandfather is 572.

Inside the adjoining wash-house it is very hot and

steamy like when you are in the bathroom a long, long time with the hot water running. There are long rows of numbered lockers with wooden benches before them. The floor is cement with little wooden slatted paths for the men to walk on as they pass bare-footed to and from the noisy showers at the building's farthest end.

"And did you have a good day today Alex?" asks my grandfather as we stop before his locker. And then unexpectedly and before I can reply he places his two big hands on either side of my head and turns it back and forth very powerfully upon my shoulders. I can feel the pressure of his calloused fingers squeezing hard against my cheeks and pressing my ears into my head and I can feel the fine, fine, coal dust which I know is covering my face and I can taste it from his thumbs which are close against my lips. It is not gritty as I had expected but is more like smoke than sand and almost like my mother's powder. And now he presses my face into his waist and holds me there for a long, long time with my nose bent over against the blackened buckle of his belt. Unable to see or hear or feel or taste or smell anything that is not black; holding me there engulfed and drowning in blackness until I am unable to breathe.

And my father is saying from a great distance: "What are you doing? Let him go! He'll suffocate." And then the big hands come away from my ears and my father's voice is louder and he sounds like my mother.

Now I am so black that I am almost afraid to move and the two men are standing over me looking into one another's eyes. "Oh, well," says my grandfather turning reluctantly toward his locker and beginning to open his shirt.

"I guess there is only one thing to do now," says my father quietly and he bends down slowly and pulls loose the laces of my shoes. Soon I am standing naked upon the wooden slats and my grandfather is the same beside me and then he guides and follows me along the wooden path that leads us to the showers and away from where my father sits. I look back once and see him sitting all alone on the bench which he has covered with his newspaper so that his suit will not be soiled.

When I come to the door of the vast shower room I hesitate because for a moment I feel afraid but I feel my grandfather strong and hairy behind me and we venture out into the pouring water and the lathered, shouting bodies and the cakes of skidding yellow soap. We cannot find a shower at first until one of my uncles shouts to us and a soap-covered man points us in the right direction. We are already wet and the blackness of my grandfather's face is running down in two grey rivulets from the corners of his moustache.

My uncle at first steps out of the main stream but then the three of us stand and move and wash beneath the torrent that spills upon us. The soap is very yellow and strong. It smells like the men's washroom in the Montreal Forum and my grandfather tells me not to get it in my eyes. Before we leave he gradually turns off the hot water and increases the cold. He says this is so we will not catch cold when we leave. It gets colder and colder but he tells me to stay under it as long as I can and I am covered with goose pimples and my teeth are chattering when I jump out for the last time. We walk back through the washing men who are not so numerous now. Then along the wooden path and I look at the tracks our bare feet leave behind.

My father is still sitting on the bench by himself as we had left him. He is glad to see us return, and smiles. My grandfather takes two heavy towels out of his locker and after we are dry he puts on his clean clothes and I put on the only ones I have except the bedraggled tie which my father stuffs into his pocket. So we go out into the sun and walk up the long, long hill and I am allowed to carry the lunch pail with the thermos bottle rattling inside. We walk very slowly and say very little. Every once in a while my grandfather stops and turns to look back the way we have come. It is very beautiful. The sun is moving into the sea as if it is tired and the sea is very blue and very wide – wide enough it seems for a hundred suns. It touches the sand of the beach which is a slender boundary of gold separating the blue from the greenness of the grass which comes rolling down upon it. Then there is the mine silhouetted against it all, looking like a toy from a meccano set; yet its bells ring as the coal-laden cars fly up out of the deep, grumble as they are unloaded, and flee with thundering power down the slopes they leave behind. Then the blackened houses begin and march row and row up the hill to where we stand and beyond to where we go. Overhead the gulls are flying inland, slowly but steadily as if they are somehow very sure of everything. My grandfather says they always fly inland in the evening. They have done so as long as he can remember.

And now we are entering the yard and my mother is rushing toward me and pressing me to her and saying to everyone and no one, "Where has this child been all day? He has not been here since morning and has eaten nothing. I have been almost out of my mind." She buries her fingers in my hair and I feel very sorry for my mother because I think she loves me very much. "Playing," I say.

At supper I am so tired that I can hardly sit up at the table and my father takes me to bed before it is yet completely dark. I wake up once when I hear my parents talking softly at my door. "I am trying very hard. I really am," says my mother. "Yes, yes I know you are," says my father gently and they move off down the hall.

And now it is in the morning two weeks later and the train that takes us back will be leaving very soon. All our suitcases are in the taxi and the good-byes are almost all completed. I am the last to leave my grandmother as she stands beside her stove. She lifts me up as she did the first night and says, "Good-bye Alex, you are the only grandchild I will never know," and presses into my hand the crinkled dollar that is never spent.

My grandfather is not in although he has not gone to work and they say he has walked on ahead of us to the station. We bump down the hill to where the train is waiting beside the small brown building and he is on the platform talking with some other men and spitting tobacco over the side.

He walks over to us and everyone says good-bye at once. I am again the last and he shakes hands very formally this time. "Good-bye Alex," he says, "it was ten years before you saw me. In another ten I will not be here to see." And then I get on the train and none too soon for already it is beginning to move. Everyone waves but the train goes on because it must and it does not care for waving. From very far away I see my grandfather turn and begin walking back up his hill. And then there is nothing but the creak and sway of the coach and the blue sea with its gulls and the green hills with the gashes of their coal imbedded deeply in their sides. And we do not say anything but sit silent and alone. We have come from a great distance and have a long way now to go.

FIVE

The Golden Gift of Grey

A T MIDNIGHT he looked up at the neon Coca-Cola clock and realized with a taut emptiness that he had already stayed too late and perhaps was even now forever lost. He lowered his eyes and then quickly raised them again with the rather desperate hope that he might on a second try somehow catch the clock by surprise and find the hands somewhere else, at nine or ten perhaps, but it was no use. There they were, perfectly vertical, like a rigid arrow of accusation seeming to condemn by their very rigidity and righteousness everything in the world that was not so straight and stern as they themselves.

He felt sick at first and almost numb along his arms and down through his wrists and into his fingers, the way he had felt the time he had been knocked out in the high school football game. He moved his shoulders beneath his shirt in an attempt to shake off the chill and ran his tongue nervously over his lips and travelled his eyes then around the pool table to the men with the cue-sticks in their hands and to the stained black-brown wood that framed the table's squareness. There were three quarters on the wood indicating that three challengers still remained. And he looked then at the soft, velvet green of the table itself, that held him, he thought, like a lotus land, and finally to the blackness of the eight-ball and the whiteness of the cue, good and evil he thought, paradoxically flowering here on the greenness of this plain. He was in his first real game, and it had somehow become a series of games, a marathon that had begun at eight when he had paused, books in hand at the doorway, and it had gone on and on, the night's hours fleeing with the swiftness and unreality of a dream. The type of dream that holds you in a delicate tensile web, even while a certain part of you knows that you will not remember in the morning, and you do not quite know if the feeling is one of ecstasy or pain, or if the awakening is victory or defeat, or if you are forever saved or yet forever doomed.

And now a voice said, "Boy, you goen to wait all night? I ain't got time." And he moved with a jolt, out of the dream but in it, and said, "Side pocket," indicating the direction with his head, and taking the cue he leaned over and across the table, raising his right leg and feeling his belt buckle press into his stomach, and the brown-black wood strong against his testicles and then the sensation of the smoothly polished wood running slickly through his fingers as he shot and then watched the gently nudged eight-ball roll softly and silently across the field of green until it vanished quietly before his eyes, and he could hear it then, changing and rolling noisily now somewhere beneath and within the table on its clattering way to join its predecessors in an underworld of dark. And then he saw the green dollar bill flutter down to the table before his eyes and even as he reached for it, someone else was pushing one of the quarters into the slot and redeeming the balls from their cavern and preparing to arrange them within the rack. And it was now after midnight and he knew he had stayed too long.

He had not been home since before eight that morning when he had walked out into the early October sunshine with his books beneath his arm. He could see the books now lying just inside the door on the end of the narrow bench that ran along the wall. They were covered defensively by his jacket and from beneath the sleeve he could see the algebra, and the red-covered geometry into which he had pencilled his marks, 90's mostly, and the English text whose poems he had almost totally committed to memory. They looked incongruous in this setting and he vaguely wished that somehow he could cover them more adequately; to protect them and perhaps to protect himself from the questions that they asked and the questions that the men might ask about them. He flicked his eyes nervously down the canyon-like room. It was long and narrow and he could hardly discern the far end with its hazy EXIT sign because of the tobacco smoke that seemed to hang in wavering layers in the stale and sour air. A long uneven bar ran almost the total length of the room, beginning near the pool table and stretching like a trackless narrow-gauge railway toward a distant bandstand where two guitarist-singers and a drummer perspired beneath the ever-changing coloured lights and blasted the heavy air with the twanging heart-break sound of Nashville. On the bar itself three bloated no-longer-young go-go girls moved with heavy unimaginative movements, their net-stockinged feet not always avoiding the sad little puddles of spilled beer. Beneath them and along the bar the men they were supposed to entertain looked up at them dutifully and wearily, although one with hair of snow moved his heavy, calloused hand rhythmically up and down the neck of his beer bottle with a slow and thoughtful masturbating motion.

Over everything and all of them the odour hung and covered and pressed like the roof of a gigantic invisible tent from which there could be no escape. It smelled of work clothes, soaked and dried in sweat and seldom washed, and of spilled beer and of the sour rags used to mop it up, and of the damp and decaying wood that lay beneath the floor, and of the reek that issued forth from the constantly swinging doors of the men's washroom: the exhausted urine and the powerful disinfectant and the shreds of tobacco and soggy cigarette papers which appeared in the trough beneath the crudely lettered signs: This is *not* an ashtray; Please don't throw cigarette butts in

our toilet, we don't urinate in your ashtray; DON'T THROW
CIGARETTE BUTTS HERE.

And as it all assailed his senses he felt that everything
was wrong with his life and that all of it was ruined,
though he was yet but in his eighteenth year. And he
wished that he were home.

He could see the situation at home now. The five
younger children would be in bed and his sister Mary, who
was sixteen, would be helping his mother prepare the
lunch that his father would carry in his pail to the meat-
packing plant. His younger brother, Donny, who was thir-
teen, would be desperately hoping, though he knew his
hopes were doomed, that the television might remain on
longer. And his father who had been propped in front of
the television in his undershirt, and in his sock feet and
with the waistband of his trousers undone, and with his
greying reddish head flopping occasionally from side to
side as he dozed and slept more than he dared admit,
would have risen and gone to lock the door for the night.
And then he would stop and ask gruffly, "Where's Jesse?"
And then there would be the awful, awkward silence, and,
"Well don't he live here no more?" And they would all
squirm and his mother would dry glasses that were
already dry, and Mary and Donny would glance furtively
at one another, while the heavy-set man, now fully awake
and puffing on his pipe, would walk from one window to
the next, shielding his eyes against the glass while trying to
catch a glimpse of his eldest son approaching beneath the
street lights. He would walk ceaselessly back and forth
with the long, loping outdoor stride which he had brought
to the northern Indiana city from eastern Kentucky and
which he could not or would not change and he would
mutter: "Where is that fella?" or more strongly, "Where'n
hell's that boy at and it goen on past twelve midnight?"
And his wife would watch too, as intently but secretly, so
that her husband would not see and become more agitated
because of her awareness. And sometimes to make it bet-

ter she would lie or tell one of the young children to say, "Jesse is studyen over at Caudell's tonight with Earl. He said he wouldn't be in till late."

Then she alone bore the burden of the watching and the waiting and it was much easier then, for unlike her husband she bore her burdens silently and you did not realize that she worried at all unless you happened to catch her at an unguarded moment and saw the trace of strain about her high cheekbones and the tautness of her jaw or the tight compression of her lips. So she would say or cause others to say, "studyen at Caudell's," because if it was not the best answer it was better than any other that she knew. And she realized that her husband, even like herself, looked upon "studyen" and whatever it might entail with a deep respect not far removed from fear. For they were both of them barely literate and found even the signing of the magnificent report cards that their children triumphantly and relentlessly presented to them something of a task. Yet while they were sometimes angry and tried to be contemptuous of "book learnen" and people who were just "book smart" they encouraged both as much as they could, seeing in them a light that had never visited their darkness, but realizing that even as they fanned the flame they were losing a grip on almost all they had of life. And feeling themselves as if washed by a flood down the side of a shale-covered Kentucky mountain, clutching and grasping at twigs and roots with their hopeful fingers bloodied raw.

They had been at the base of a very real Kentucky mountain ten years ago when Everett Caudell had finally convinced them to come North. He had been a friend of the boy's father in the isolation of that squirrel-hunting, pie-social youth and their girls had become the wives they had taken with them to the anguish of the coal camps where jobs and life were at best uncertain amidst an awful certainty of poverty and pain. Caudell had come North and secured the job in the meat-packing plant and then returned with the battered half-ton truck for his family and their belongings and then again for the friend of his youth. The friend who had recently been almost killed when the roof of the illegal little mine that burrowed into the hillside had come crashing down. He had escaped only because he saw the rats racing by him toward the light and had dropped his tools and followed, sprinting after them and almost stepping on their scaly tails as the beginning roar of the crashing rock and the shot-gun pops of the snapping timbers sounded in his ears.

Ever since, both he and his wife had been more strongly religious than before because they felt somehow that God had either sent the fleeing rats as a sign or had physically propelled the man upon his way, and perhaps had even planned it so that they might come North to a new life. A life that found them ten years later waiting after midnight for the sound of footsteps at their door.

Always before, he had been home by eleven-thirty. Always. Always. But now he was here with the music and the odour in his ears and in his nose, with the cue-stick in his hand and with the green table beneath the tarnished yellow light flat before him. He could see the quarters of the challengers and hear the voices of the men quietly placing side bets behind him and he knew somehow that no matter what the cost, and almost against his soul, he would not, could not go. For it had taken him a long time to reach this night and it could never be again.

It was two years since he had first stopped outside the open door and gazed in at the life that moved beyond it. It had been a hot night in midsummer with the heat moving in little waves off the sidewalk and he had been returning from his job at the Grocery. He had been first attracted by the music, the sound of Eddy Arnold and Jim Reeves, that his father played constantly and of which both he and his sister were ashamed. They did not know the aching loneliness of which it spoke and when it floated from the windows of their house on warm summer nights it branded their parents indelibly as hillbillies and they themselves as well, as extensions of those parents. And it was a label that they hated and did not wish to bear.

He had watched, that night, fascinated, from the sidewalk and when people began to jostle him he had stood in the doorway and then with one foot inside the door, mindful of the signs that read: We do not serve minors; If you are under 21, do not enter; but entering nevertheless although with one eye always careful of the door while wearing that expression that he had often noticed on the faces of nervous gentle Negroes on the fringes of all-white crowds.

He had stopped then almost every evening for a week on his way home, standing outside or just inside the door, captured by the music and the odour but most of all by the heavy men moving around the pool table. And then one night he had looked up at the man who was then holding the cue-stick and his eyes had looked into the eyes of Everett Caudell and their glances had met and held, somewhere there in the emptiness of the space above the table like the probing, seeking beams of two lonely mountain freight trains which round a bend at midnight and find themselves even in that instant forever committed to each other. And he had sensed even then the way that it would be; that Everett Caudell would never tell his father "I seen Jesse the other night," nor would he tell Earl Caudell who was in the same grade and played football in the same backfield, "I saw your father playing pool in a bar the other night." Because some things transcend all differences in age, and chronology in the end is but an empty word.

And so he had begun. At night on the way home from the Grocery he would stop for ten or twenty minutes to watch, standing just within the door and against the wall. Always mindful of the sign which reminded him that he was a "minor" and as such should "not enter"; but realizing with the passage of time that no one really cared, no more than they cared for the other sign which read, NO GAMBLING. And he moved farther away from the door and deeper and deeper into the room, becoming slowly aware that the strange, violent, profane men seemed to like him and winked at him when they sank the good shots and complained to him when they missed. And he discovered still later that the door was open even at four when he went to work as well as at seven when he returned. Often in the time when there was no football practice he would almost run from school to get there for a few precious moments, hoping with a desperate hope that the table would be empty and waiting so that he might deposit the quarter which was always sweaty because he held it so tightly while almost running. And then he would watch and listen to the balls as they rolled to their release and practice by himself the shots he had seen the night before; practice intently and relentlessly until four o'clock when the heavy men began to appear from the completion of their shifts. He had done all of this somehow without even daring to think that he would ever play in a real game himself, and now, seeing and feeling his body leaning over the table, he felt a strange sensation and kinship with those boys in the F. Scott Fitzgerald stories who practice and practice but never play until a certain moment comes along in their lives and changes them forever.

There had been four men playing when he had entered and taken his stand beside the wall and beneath the signs that forbade his presence. Two sets of middle-aged men who circled the table, first swiftly with their eyes and then slowly with their bodies, speaking to the balls with pleading profanity and wiping away the tiny beads of perspiration that formed upon their brows. They played for only the token dollar, which too was forbidden by a sign, and when the losers had paid, one of them said that he must go home and had gone almost instantly. And then his partner had turned and said to the figure that he had so often seen there beside the wall, "Me and you," and offered him the cue-stick. So he had taken it, almost instinctively and if feeling like the boys of Fitzgerald, feeling also, and perhaps more, like the many youths of Conrad who never thought they would do what is now already done. And the commitment had been made and the night had so begun.

At first he was so preoccupied with the thought that he would lose and have to pay a dollar he was not sure he had, that he played very badly and they won only because of the shots his partner made, but in the second and third games he became stronger, playing cautiously and deliberately and while he was not spectacular at least he did not lose and he was surprised at how much he had learned from the solitary practice sessions and from the hours of standing and watching beneath the signs. And when the men they had played went out into the darkness he and his partner played against each other and after what seemed like a very long time he won and pocketed the dollar and stayed and stayed, seeing from the corner of his eye the challenging quarters being laid on the brown-black wood by the broken-nailed fingers of the faceless unknown men, until he had recognized one set of fingers and looked into the face of Everett Caudell but said nothing, as nothing had been said on that first meeting here in a time that seemed so long ago. So they played quietly, both of them, very carefully and very slowly until only the eight-ball remained and the older man took his shot and scratched and then laid his dollar upon the table and went out into the night and was replaced by a set of nameless hands and another nameless face.

He had thought while playing against Caudell many different things. First he had been embarrassed and afraid that the man would attempt to make conversation and then he had thought, that if he were to lose, it would be very fitting that his loss should be to the only man of all those present that he really knew. And then he had, right until the end, been very much afraid that Everett Caudell would purposely lose the game, the way a fond father loses at checkers to his seven-year-old child, and he had hoped and almost prayed that they would both not have to go through such an emasculating loss of dignity on this his night of realization. And when he finally was certain that Caudell was playing his very best he felt deeply grateful for the unspoken acknowledgement and when the defeated man departed he was overcome by a mingled feeling of loneliness and sorrow, regret and anger and fierce exultant pride that made him almost ashamed. The way one feels when standing at the graveside of a loved one that has died.

And the night flashed on and he played as if still in the dream, unaddled by the beer that began to affect his opponents with the hours passing and unaddled by the music or the activities that became more frenzied as the night wore on. Once he had raised his head, to the twanging bass chords of a Duane Eddy composition, and looked along the bar's surface where one of the perspiring middle-aged dancers spread her heavy net-stockinged limbs and lowered herself gradually and gradually until she was almost sitting on the bald head of the man who had leaned forward across the bar, holding him there with a hot, heavy inner thigh against each of his ears and grinding herself backwards and forwards across the baldness of his pate. And he had felt almost sick then and had quickly averted his eyes and taken his shot too quickly and missed.

At one-thirty a man tapped him on the shoulder and told him someone wanted to speak to him and he had turned to see his younger brother, Donny, beckoning him from the street through the door that was still open. He excused himself and went out quickly, pulling the solid door behind him so powerfully that it slammed, as if by doing so he protected his brother from the woman on the bar and perhaps himself from the men within.

Donny's brown eyes were wide in their sockets and he began to speak in fast little uneven sentences: "Gee, you better come home. They're walking around looking out the windows. It's awful, especially Dad. He's smoking like mad. He's got that funny look on his face. They don't know where you're at."

At first he was afraid but he tried to act amused. "Look, what's the difference? I'm too late now. I might as well stay out all night eh?"

"But Jesse, you know what it'll be like when you come home."

"So? Will it be any worse in the morning?" The look on Donny's face plainly indicated that it would.

"Jesse, what will I tell them?"

"Tell them I'm playing pool."

"They don't know what pool is and what if they ask where?"

"Tell them."

"Jesse, you're nuts. The old man will be down here in five minutes if he knows. You know what he's like. There's no telling what he'll do."

He thought then of the awful violence that was within his father; a something that rumbled deep below like some subterranean mountain stream of roaring white water, splashing and pounding dark rocks within deep unseen caves. He remembered seeing it only once as a child, in Hazard or Harlan and he could not now remember which, the man his father had hit, literally flying like a grotesque rag doll across the space of the behind-the-store parking lot and how he had lain there so crumpled and still for so long with the blood trickling past his broken teeth in slender, threadlike, crimson streams. And his mother had prayed, "O Lord may this man not die, I'm asken you." And his father had buried his head within his arms and leaned against the wall of the store, perhaps praying too while his fists remained so tightly clenched that the knuckles showed white, as if he were trying to hang on to something very desperately but was uncertain what it was. And after a while they, as children, cried too, because they knew there was something wrong but did not know what else to do.

Behind him now, the door opened and as he turned he saw the dancers again along the bar, and the man framed in the doorway saying, "you goen to finish this game? I ain't got time," and he started nervously and said to Donny, "Look, I gotta go. Make up your own story. Tell them I'm okay. I'll be home later." As he turned to the building he averted his eyes from his brother's face in order to avoid the tears that he sensed but did not wish to see.

So he went back in and thought of how Donny was the greatest little brother in the world. Of how he had never broken any of his brother's confidences, of how he would spend hours shining that brother's shoes or running faithfully after the baseballs he lofted into the skies and of how when the brother had first started smoking he would go all over town like a tireless little robot gathering bottles until he had acquired enough for the precious package of cigarettes. Sometimes he had the feeling that if he told Donny to walk off the edge of a towering building he would do so without a moment's hesitation and the thought of the awful power seemed to tighten around his heart.

At three he left the bar that had officially closed at two and felt that he had no place to go. It was both too late and too early to go home. He went into the street and then entered an alley and stood in the darkness, listening to the scuffle of the rats and waiting for the dawn; he shivered in the cold and tried to think of what he would say if anyone should come along and see him standing there, shivering in an alley with his books beneath his arm. Almost fearfully he backed into the shadow of a building and shoved his hands into the pockets of his trousers. It was then that he felt the money and jumped as if he had been shocked. He had been so intent on playing that he had forgotten about the dollar bills he had been pocketing. But now he felt them in two tangled, crumpled lumps. Lumps that were now a chilly damp, but had once been warm and almost soggy from the perspiration of his thighs. He tried to count them without light and without taking them from his pockets, fingering what he thought was a new corner, and then another, and counting the corners of one pocket and then the other, and finally in despair, because he never got the same number twice, giving it up altogether and starting suddenly back into the street.

When he entered the all-night coffee shop he sat on the second last stool and laid his books on the very last, hoping that he would not be noticed there and that he might have at least some privacy. The cloth of his trousers pulled tight against his thighs when he sat and he could feel and sense the protruding of the pockets' bulges, knowing what they looked like without even looking down, and afraid to look down lest his worst fears be confirmed, or that by so doing he should draw attention to something he had no wish to publicize. Thinking it was like the mysterious coming of the ill-timed adolescent erection, when one knows that it is there, unbidden and unwanted and unbecomingly wrong.

He ordered the coffee and then slowly drew the crumpled bills from the right pocket. Probably, he thought, because he was right-handed. One by one he uncrumpled and flattened them. They were still damp and smelled faintly of salt. There were nineteen. Then he did the same with the contents of the left. There were twelve. Thirty-one dollars.

He left the coffee shop with the bills neatly folded in the breast-pocket of his shirt and with his mood completely changed. He would go home and he would give it to them he thought. It would be the first worthwhile gift that he would give to those from whom he had always taken. And he was filled with a great love for the strange people that were his parents. Parents whom he found so difficult to understand, who still made treks to Kentucky and who were not above being openly emotional when their battered old car crossed the mighty bridge from Cincinnati to Covington, and who would not wash the red hill mud from that car on their return, waiting for the rains to do so as it stood out in the yard, and who listened always to their hillbilly music.

And he was ashamed now of the times he had been

ashamed of them. He remembered the awful experience of the "Parents' Night" when he had been in fourth grade, the year after the move, and of how he had wildly begged them to accompany him to view the wonders of his school, and of how they themselves had become even mildly excited and had washed and scrubbed themselves to redness in anticipation of the big event. Once inside the great building, however, what natural dignity they possessed had seemed to drain from them immediately, as if some magic stoppers had been pulled beneath their shoes. And they had become blank and dumb and very nearly overcome by panic in that strange foreign world of animated numerals and foot-high ABC's and posters that told one how to do everything it seemed, from brushing one's teeth to crossing at street corners to feeding birds in winter. His mother had said, "Mighty fine," "This sure is mighty fine," "It sure is mighty fine," over and over again as if her mind were locked in a groove, and his father's line, while crushing his hat in his massive hands, had been, "Ah sure do appreciate all this here," and he had said it indiscriminately, to teachers, to other parents and to janitors alike. And in the eyes of Miss Downs, the fourth-grade teacher, he had seen the unspoken question: "How can such a bright little boy as Jesse have parents such as these?" He remembered now that he had rather wondered how, himself.

At five-forty-five he went home after stopping at an all-night service station to convert thirty-one dollar bills into a twenty and a ten. Everybody was up; his mother was getting breakfast although it was too early; the table was set and his father's lunch pail lay open on its side. No one said a word, and he had a strange feeling that he had gone deaf. He had never thought the house could be so quiet. He looked at his mother, but she kept her eyes on the stove, and then he looked at Donny who seemed about to burst into tears.

And then it was like the beginning of a play in which his father had the first lines, "And where the hell have you been?" Lines that came out clear and well rehearsed, as if he had been practicing and practicing, and they were not loud nor hard as he had expected. And he – he had not rehearsed, he had not studied his lines well enough, but he stumbled out into the middle of the stage and began to take his part, and a voice within him said, "Tell him the truth," and the peculiar unrehearsed voice said, "I was playing pool."

"We have been waiting for you all night," said his mother evenly, sounding the endings to all her words, "we thought something had happened to you, that you'd been beaten or that you'd been robbed."

He was very happy suddenly and filled with love because of their concern. His voice said excitedly: "No, no, nothing happened. I didn't lose anything. I won. Look!" And he began to withdraw the thirty-one dollars from his pocket. Someone said, "How much?" and he almost laughed and said, "Thirty-one dollars," drawing the gift completely from his pocket and laying it on the table.

His mother said, "Before you have a bite of breakfast in this house, go and give it back."

He was stopped then in full tilt and almost crushed, as if he were bolting for the hole in the football line and suddenly found that the daylight had vanished and the hole had closed and the opposition's weight was squeezing out his life.

And then he was angry and shouted, "Give it back? Who to?"

And his mother said, still evenly, "To the people you took it from. The Lord has been good to us and it seems He wouldn't want none of this."

He burst into tears of anger and sorrow and hopelessness, and tried to explain: "But you don't understand. The Lord has nothing to do with it. I didn't steal it. It's mine. I won it. I can't give it back. I don't even know their names."

His father said, "You heard your mother," so he

stormed out of the house and stood at the gate, crying, until Donny came out and he was forced to stop. In his pocket his hand clutched the little ball that was now the thirty-one dollars, three bills that were soaked from the sweat of his perspiring palms. He looked at the sleeping soon-to-be-awakened city and did not know what to do.

He started to walk then but soon he was running. Down several streets and across several others in the almost-light of early morning. He slowed down just as he entered the Caudells' yard, trying to walk slowly as if just out for a stroll, though breathing heavily.

He found Everett Caudell in the kitchen, sitting by himself with a cup of coffee and listening to his little radio as it valiantly tried to pull in the fast-fading signal from Wheeling, West Virginia. The others were still in bed and he himself was not completely dressed, being still in his stockinged feet, and with his heavy shirt yet unbuttoned and his trousers not yet firmly fastened by the broadness of his heavy belt.

"How do, Jesse?" he said as casually as if he had been whittling a stick on his doorstep in the middle of a Sunday afternoon. "How ya bin? Coffee?"

He was surprised first because he hadn't been asked why he was about at such an hour but the surprise was short-lived and soon buried beneath the avalanche of his reason for coming. "Here," he said, pulling the three criminal, sweat-stained bills from his pocket and thrusting them at the man, "here, take them. They're for you – you lost last night."

The big man said kindly: "Take it easy lad. Sit down now. What's all this? What's all this?" and he began to fill his pipe as if there were all the time in the world and the world were never to end. And the words tumbled out then, one after the other, on top of one another, passed and thundered and banged one against the other, like the coal when it comes bounding down the chutes, which was one of the few images he remembered from Kentucky, crashing and rolling and pounding, in big lumps and little ones, and the big being broken into the small, and he ended saying: "I've got to give it to someone, and it's for you because you lost and I won – and I shouldn't have."

The man took them then, the three dirty bills, the twenty, the ten and the one, and put them in the pocket of his still unbuttoned shirt. "Aye lad," he said, "your father is a good man and your mother a good woman; now go on back and tell them what you've done, and if they come to me, why I'll tell them, 'Sure, he give it to me, a twenty, a ten, and a one,' just like you did."

When he was at the door he heard his name immediately behind him and turned to find that Caudell had followed him on silent stockinged feet and was now standing directly in front of him. And then before he could move he saw the older man quickly and quietly tuck the three bills into the shirt pocket of his guest. "Now there," he said, "there ain't nothen wrong. There's no lie. You give it to me and I took it. We'll leave it be like that. Now go on home as I hear the army starten to move upstairs."

And he went out then into the new day and after a while he even whistled a bit, and he thought of how he'dknock the geometry exam dead next week and of how the football pads would settle with familiar friendliness upon his waiting shoulders that very afternoon. Already he could sense the shouts and hand-claps from the sun-drenched field and as he began to jog, he could hear the golden leaves as they turned beneath his feet.

SIX

The Boat

T HERE ARE times even now, when I awake at four
o'clock in the morning with the terrible fear that I
have overslept; when I imagine that my father is waiting
for me in the room below the darkened stairs or that the
shorebound men are tossing pebbles against my window
while blowing their hands and stomping their feet impatiently on the frozen steadfast earth. There are times when
I am half out of bed and fumbling for socks and mum-
bling for words before I realize that I am foolishly alone,
that no one waits at the base of the stairs and no boat rides
restlessly in the waters by the pier.

At such times only the grey corpses on the overflowing
ashtray beside my bed bear witness to the extinction of the
latest spark and silently await the crushing out of the most
recent of their fellows. And then because I am afraid to be
alone with death, I dress rapidly, make a great to-do about
clearing my throat, turn on both faucets in the sink and
proceed to make loud splashing ineffectual noises. Later I
go out and walk the mile to the all-night restaurant.

In the winter it is a very cold walk and there are often
tears in my eyes when I arrive. The waitress usually gives
a sympathetic little shiver and says, "Boy, it must be really
cold out there; you got tears in your eyes."

"Yes," I say, "it sure is; it really is."

And then the three or four of us who are always in such
places at such times make uninteresting little protective

chit-chat until the dawn reluctantly arrives. Then I swallow the coffee which is always bitter and leave with a great busy rush because by that time I have to worry about being late and whether I have a clean shirt and whether my car will start and about all the other countless things one must worry about when he teaches at a great Midwestern university. And I know then that that day will go by as have all the days of the past ten years, for the call and the voices and the shapes and the boat were not really there in the early morning's darkness and I have all kinds of comforting reality to prove it. They are only shadows and echoes, the animals a child's hands make on the wall by lamplight, and the voices from the rain barrel; the cuttings from an old movie made in the black and white of long ago.

I first became conscious of the boat in the same way and at almost the same time that I became aware of the people it supported. My earliest recollection of my father is a view from the floor of gigantic rubber boots and then of being suddenly elevated and having my face pressed against the stubble of his cheek, and of how it tasted of salt and of how he smelled of salt from his red-soled rubber boots to the shaggy whiteness of his hair.

When I was very small, he took me for my first ride in the boat. I rode the half-mile from our house to the wharf on his shoulders and I remember the sound of his rubber boots galumphing along the gravel beach, the tune of the indecent little song he used to sing, and the odour of the salt.

The floor of the boat was permeated with the same odour and in its constancy I was not aware of change. In the harbour we made our little circle and returned. He tied the boat by its painter, fastened the stern to its permanent anchor and lifted me high over his head to the solidity of the wharf. Then he climbed up the little iron ladder that led to the wharf's cap, placed me once more upon his shoulders and galumphed off again.

When we returned to the house everyone made a great

fuss over my precocious excursion and asked, "How did you like the boat?" "Were you afraid in the boat?" "Did you cry in the boat?" They repeated "the boat" at the end of all their questions and I knew it must be very important to everyone.

My earliest recollection of my mother is of being alone with her in the mornings while my father was away in the boat. She seemed to be always repairing clothes that were "torn in the boat," preparing food "to be eaten in the boat" or looking for "the boat" through our kitchen window which faced upon the sea. When my father returned about noon, she would ask, "Well, how did things go in the boat today?" It was the first question I remember asking: "Well, how did things go in the boat today?" "Well, how did things go in the boat today?"

The boat in our lives was registered at Port Hawkesbury. She was what Nova Scotians called a Cape Island boat and was designed for the small inshore fishermen who sought the lobsters of the spring and the mackerel of summer and later the cod and haddock and hake. She was thirty-two feet long and nine wide, and was powered by an engine from a Chevrolet truck. She had a marine clutch and a high speed reverse gear and was painted light green with the name *Jenny Lynn* stencilled in black letters on her bow and painted on an oblong plate across her stern. Jenny Lynn had been my mother's maiden name and the boat was called after her as another link in the chain of tradition. Most of the boats that berthed at the wharf bore the names of some female member of their owner's household.

I say this now as if I knew it all then. All at once, all about boat dimensions and engines, and as if on the day of my first childish voyage I noticed the difference between a stencilled name and a painted name. But of course it was not that way at all, for I learned it all very slowly and there was not time enough.

I learned first about our house which was one of about fifty which marched around the horseshoe of our harbour and the wharf which was its heart. Some of them were so close to the water that during a storm the sea spray splashed against their windows while others were built farther along the beach as was the case with ours. The houses and their people, like those of the neighbouring towns and villages, were the result of Ireland's discontent and Scotland's Highland Clearances and America's War of Independence. Impulsive emotional Catholic Celts who could not bear to live with England and shrewd determined Protestant Puritans who, in the years after 1776, could not bear to live without.

The most important room in our house was one of those oblong old-fashioned kitchens heated by a wood-and coal-burning stove. Behind the stove was a box of kindlings and beside it a coal scuttle. A heavy wooden table with leaves that expanded or reduced its dimensions stood in the middle of the floor. There were five wooden homemade chairs which had been chipped and hacked by a variety of knives. Against the east wall, opposite the stove, there was a couch which sagged in the middle and had a cushion for a pillow, and above it a shelf which contained matches, tobacco, pencils, odd fish-hooks, bits of twine, and a tin can filled with bills and receipts. The south wall was dominated by a window which faced the sea and on the north there was a five-foot board which bore a variety of clothes hooks and the burdens of each. Beneath the board there was a jumble of odd footwear, mostly of rubber. There was also, on this wall, a barometer, a map of the marine area and a shelf which held a tiny radio. The kitchen was shared by all of us and was a buffer zone between the immaculate order of ten other rooms and the disruptive chaos of the single room that was my father's.

My mother ran her house as her brothers ran their boats. Everything was clean and spotless and in order. She was tall and dark and powerfully energetic. In later years she reminded me of the women of Thomas Hardy, particularly Eustacia Vye, in a physical way. She fed and clothed a family of seven children, making all of the meals and most of the clothes. She grew miraculous gardens and magnificent flowers and raised broods of hens and ducks. She would walk miles on berry-picking expeditions and hoist her skirts to dig for clams when the tide was low. She was fourteen years younger than my father, whom she had married when she was twenty-six and had been a local beauty for a period of ten years. My mother was of the sea as were all of her people, and her horizons were the very literal ones she scanned with her dark and fearless eyes.

Between the kitchen clothes rack and barometer, a door opened into my father's bedroom. It was a room of disorder and disarray. It was as if the wind which so often clamoured about the house succeeded in entering this single room and after whipping it into turmoil stole quietly away to renew its knowing laughter from without.

My father's bed was against the south wall. It always looked rumpled and unmade because he lay on top of it more than he slept within any folds it might have had. Beside it, there was a little brown table. An archaic goose-necked reading light, a battered table radio, a mound of wooden matches, one or two packages of tobacco, a deck of cigarette papers and an overflowing ashtray cluttered its surface. The brown larvae of tobacco shreds and the grey flecks of ash covered both the table and the floor beneath it. The once-varnished surface of the table was disfigured by numerous black scars and gashes inflicted by the neglected burning cigarettes of many years. They had tumbled from the ashtray unnoticed and branded their statements permanently and quietly into the wood until the odour of their burning caused the snuffing out of their lives. At the bed's foot there was a single window which looked upon the sea.

Against the adjacent wall there was a battered bureau and beside it there was a closet which held his single ill-fitting serge suit, the two or three white shirts that strangled him and the square black shoes that pinched. When he took off his more friendly clothes, the heavy woollen sweaters, mitts and socks which my mother knitted for him and the woollen and doeskin shirts, he dumped them unceremoniously on a single chair. If a visitor entered the room while he was lying on the bed, he would be told to throw the clothes on the floor and take their place upon the chair.

Magazines and books covered the bureau and competed with the clothes for domination of the chair. They further overburdened the heroic little table and lay on top of the radio. They filled a baffling and unknowable cave beneath the bed, and in the corner by the bureau they spilled from the walls and grew up from the floor.

The magazines were the most conventional: *Time, Newsweek, Life, Maclean's Family Herald, Reader's Digest*. They were the result of various cut-rate subscriptions or of the gift subscriptions associated with Christmas, "the two whole years for only $3.50."

The books were more varied. There were a few hardcover magnificents and bygone Book-of-the-Month wonders and some were Christmas or birthday gifts. The majority of them, however, were used paperbacks which came from those second-hand bookstores which advertise in the backs of magazines: "Miscellaneous Used Paperbacks 10¢ Each." At first he sent for them himself, although my mother resented the expense, but in later years they came more and more often from my sisters who had moved to the cities. Especially at first they were very weird and varied. Mickey Spillane and Ernest Haycox vied with Dostoyevsky and Faulkner, and the Penguin Poets edition of Gerard Manley Hopkins arrived in the same box as a little book on sex technique called *Getting the Most Out of Love*. The former had been assiduously annotated by a very fine hand using a very blue-inked fountain pen while the latter had been studied by someone with very large thumbs, the prints of which were still visible in the margins. At the slightest provocation it would open almost automatically to particularly graphic and well-smudged pages.

When he was not in the boat, my father spent most of his time lying on the bed in his socks, the top two buttons of his trousers undone, his discarded shirt on the ever-ready chair and the sleeves of the woollen Stanfield underwear, which he wore both summer and winter, drawn half way up to his elbows. The pillows propped up the whiteness of his head and the goose-necked lamp illuminated the pages in his hands. The cigarettes smoked and smouldered on the ashtray and on the table and the radio played constantly, sometimes low and sometimes loud. At midnight and at one, two, three and four, one could sometimes hear the radio, his occasional cough, the rustling thud of a completed book being tossed to the corner heap, or the movement necessitated by his sitting on the edge of the bed to roll the thousandth cigarette. He seemed never to sleep, only to doze, and the light shone constantly from his window to the sea.

My mother despised the room and all it stood for and she had stopped sleeping in it after I was born. She despised disorder in rooms and in houses and in hours and in lives, and she had not read a book since high school. There she had read *Ivanhoe* and considered it a colossal waste of time. Still the room remained, like a rock of opposition in the sparkling waters of a clear deep harbour, opening off the kitchen where we really lived our lives, with its door always open and its contents visible to all.

The daughters of the room and of the house were very beautiful. They were tall and willowy like my mother and had her fine facial features set off by the reddish copper-coloured hair that had apparently once been my father's before it turned to white. All of them were very clever in school and helped my mother a great deal about the house. When they were young they sang and were very happy and very nice to me because I was the youngest and the family's only boy.

My father never approved of their playing about the wharf like the other children, and they went there only when my mother sent them on an errand. At such times they almost always overstayed, playing screaming games of tag or hide-and-seek in and about the fishing shanties, the piled traps and tubs of trawl, shouting down to the perch that swam languidly about the wharf's algae-covered piles, or jumping in and out of the boats that tugged gently at their lines. My mother was never uneasy about them at such times, and when her husband criticized her she would say, "Nothing will happen to them there," or "They could be doing worse things in worse places."

By about the ninth or tenth grade my sisters one by one discovered my father's bedroom and then the change would begin. Each would go into the room one morning when he was out. She would go with the ideal hope of imposing order or with the more practical objective of emptying the ashtray, and later she would be found spellbound by the volume in her hand. My mother's reaction was always abrupt, bordering on the angry. "Take your nose out of that trash and come and do your work," she would say, and once I saw her slap my youngest sister so hard that the print of her hand was scarletly emblazoned upon her daughter's cheek while the broken-spined paperback fluttered uselessly to the floor.

Thereafter my mother would launch a campaign against what she had discovered but could not understand. At times although she was not overly religious she would bring in God to bolster her arguments, saying, "In the next world God will see to those who waste their lives reading useless books when they should be about their work." Or without theological aid, "I would like to know how books help anyone to live a life." If my father were in, she would repeat the remarks louder than necessary, and her voice would carry into his room where he lay upon his bed. His usual reaction was to turn up the volume of the radio, although that action in itself betrayed the success of the initial thrust.

Shortly after my sisters began to read the books, they grew restless and lost interest in darning socks and baking bread, and all of them eventually went to work as summer waitresses in the Sea Food Restaurant. The restaurant was run by a big American concern from Boston and catered to the tourists that flooded the area during July and August. My mother despised the whole operation. She said the restaurant was not run by "our people," and "our people" did not eat there, and that it was run by outsiders for outsiders.

"Who are these people anyway?" she would ask, tossing back her dark hair, "and what do they, though they go about with their cameras for a hundred years, know about the way it is here, and what do they care about me and mine, and why should I care about them?"

She was angry that my sisters should even conceive of working in such a place and more angry when my father made no move to prevent it, and she was worried about herself and about her family and about her life. Sometimes she would say softly to her sisters, "I don't know what's the matter with my girls. It seems none of them are interested in any of the right things." And sometimes there would be bitter savage arguments. One afternoon I was coming in with three mackerel I'd been given at the wharf when I heard her say, "Well I hope you'll be satisfied when they come home knocked up and you'll have had your way."

It was the most savage thing I'd ever heard my mother say. Not just the words but the way she said them, and I stood there in the porch afraid to breathe for what seemed like the years from ten to fifteen, feeling the damp moist mackerel with their silver glassy eyes growing clammy against my leg.

Through the angle in the screen door I saw my father who had been walking into his room wheel around on one of his rubber-booted heels and look at her with his blue eyes flashing like clearest ice beneath the snow that was his hair. His usually ruddy face was drawn and grey, reflecting the exhaustion of a man of sixty-five who had been working in those rubber boots for eleven hours on an August day, and for a fleeting moment I wondered what I would do if he killed my mother while I stood there in the porch with those three foolish mackerel in my hand. Then he turned and went into his room and the radio blared forth the next day's weather forecast and I retreated under the noise and returned again, stamping my feet and slamming the door too loudly to signal my approach. My mother was busy at the stove when I came in, and did not raise her head when I threw the mackerel in a pan. As I looked into my father's room, I said, "Well how did things go in the boat today?" and he replied, "Oh not too badly, all things considered." He was lying on his back and lighting the first cigarette and the radio was talking about the Virginia coast.

All of my sisters made good money on tips. They bought my father an electric razor which he tried to use for a while and they took out even more magazine subscriptions. They bought my mother a great many clothes of the type she was very fond of, the wide-brimmed hats and the brocaded dresses, but she locked them all in trunks and refused to wear any of them.

On one August day my sisters prevailed upon my father to take some of their restaurant customers for an afternoon ride in the boat. The tourists with their expensive clothes and cameras and sun glasses awkwardly backed down the iron ladder at the wharf's side to where my father waited below, holding the rocking *Jenny Lynn* in snug against the wharf with one hand on the iron ladder and steadying his descending passengers with the other. They tried to look both prim and wind-blown like the girls in the Pepsi-Cola ads and did the best they could, sitting on the thwarts where the newspapers were spread to cover the splattered blood and fish entrails, crowding to one side so that they were in danger of capsizing the boat, taking the inevitable pictures or merely trailing their fingers through the water of their dreams.

All of them liked my father very much and, after he'd brought them back from their circles in the harbour, they invited him to their rented cabins which were located high on a hill overlooking the village to which they were so alien. He proceeded to get very drunk up there with the beautiful view and the strange company and the abundant liquor, and late in the afternoon he began to sing.

I was just approaching the wharf to deliver my mother's summons when he began, and the familiar yet unfamiliar voice that rolled down from the cabins made me feel as I had never felt before in my young life or perhaps as I had always felt without really knowing it, and I was ashamed yet proud, young yet old and saved yet forever lost, and there was nothing I could do to control my legs which trembled nor my eyes which wept for what they could not tell.

The tourists were equipped with tape recorders and my father sang for more than three hours. His voice boomed down the hill and bounced off the surface of the harbour, which was an unearthly blue on that hot August day, and was then reflected to the wharf and the fishing shanties where it was absorbed amidst the men who were baiting their lines for the next day's haul.

He sang all the old sea chanties which had come across from the old world and by which men like him had pulled ropes for generations, and he sang the East Coast sea songs which celebrated the sealing vessels of Northumberland Strait and the long liners of the Grand Banks, and of Anticosti, Sable Island, Grand Manan, Boston Harbor, Nantucket and Block Island. Gradually he shifted to the seemingly unending Gaelic drinking songs with their twenty or more verses and inevitable refrains, and the men in the shanties smiled at the coarseness of some of the verses and at the thought that the singer's immediate audience did not know what they were applauding nor recording to take back to staid old Boston. Later as the sun was setting he switched to the laments and the wild and haunting Gaelic war songs of those spattered Highland ancestors he had never seen, and when his voice ceased, the savage melancholy of three hundred years seemed to hang over the peaceful harbour and the quiet boats and the men leaning in the doorways of their shanties with their cigarettes glowing in the dusk and the women looking to the sea from their open windows with their children in their arms.

When he came home he threw the money he had earned on the kitchen table as he did with all his earnings but my mother refused to touch it and the next day he went with the rest of the men to bait his trawl in the shanties. The tourists came to the door that evening and my mother met them there and told them that her husband was not in although he was lying on the bed only a few feet away with the radio playing and the cigarette upon his lips. She stood in the doorway until they reluctantly went away.

In the winter they sent him a picture which had been taken on the day of the singing. On the back it said, "To Our Ernest Hemingway" and the "Our" was underlined. There was also an accompanying letter telling how much they had enjoyed themselves, how popular the tape was proving and explaining who Ernest Hemingway was. In a way it almost did look like one of those unshaven, taken-in-Cuba pictures of Hemingway. He looked both massive and incongruous in the setting. His bulky fisherman's clothes were too big for the green and white lawn chair in which he sat, and his rubber boots seemed to take up all of the well-clipped grass square. The beach umbrella jarred with his sunburned face and because he had already been singing for some time, his lips which chapped in the winds of spring and burned in the water glare of summer had already cracked in several places, producing tiny flecks of blood at their corners and on the whiteness of his teeth. The bracelets of brass chain which he wore to protect his wrists from chafing seemed abnormally large and his broad leather belt had been slackened and his heavy shirt and underwear were open at the throat revealing an uncultivated wilderness of white chest hair bordering on the semi-controlled stubble of his neck and chin. His blue eyes had looked directly into the camera and his hair was whiter than the two tiny clouds which hung over his left shoulder. The sea was behind him and its immense blue flatness stretched out to touch the arching blueness of the sky. It seemed very far away from him or else he was so much in the foreground that he seemed too big for it.

Each year another of my sisters would read the books and work in the restaurant. Sometimes they would stay out quite late on the hot summer nights and when they came up the stairs my mother would ask them many long and involved questions which they resented and tried to avoid. Before ascending the stairs they would go into my father's room and those of us who waited above could hear them throwing his clothes off the chair before sitting on it or the squeak of the bed as they sat on its edge. Sometimes they would talk to him a long time, the murmur of their voices blending with the music of the radio into a mysterious vapour-like sound which floated softly up the stairs.

I say this again as if it all happened at once and as if all of my sisters were of identical ages and like so many lemmings going into another sea and, again, it was of course not that way at all. Yet go they did, to Boston, to Montreal, to New York with the young men they met during the summers and later married in those far-away cities. The young men were very articulate and handsome and wore fine clothes and drove expensive cars and my sisters, as I said, were very tall and beautiful with their copper-coloured hair and were tired of darning socks and baking bread.

One by one they went. My mother had each of her daughters for fifteen years, then lost them for two and finally forever. None married a fisherman. My mother never accepted any of the young men, for in her eyes they seemed always a combination of the lazy, the effeminate, the dishonest and the unknown. They never seemed to do any physical work and she could not comprehend their luxurious vacations and she did not know whence they came nor who they were. And in the end she did not really care, for they were not of her people and they were not of her sea.

I say this now with a sense of wonder at my own stupidity in thinking I was somehow free and would go on doing well in school and playing and helping in the boat and passing into my early teens while streaks of grey began to appear in my mother's dark hair and my father's rubber boots dragged sometimes on the pebbles of the beach as he trudged home from the wharf. And there were but three of us in the house that had at one time been so loud.

Then during the winter that I was fifteen he seemed to grow old and ill at once. Most of January he lay upon the bed, smoking and reading and listening to the radio while the wind howled about the house and the needle-like snow blistered off the ice-covered harbour and the doors flew out of people's hands if they did not cling to them like death.

In February when the men began overhauling their lobster traps he still did not move, and my mother and I began to knit lobster trap headings in the evenings. The twine was as always very sharp and harsh, and blisters formed upon our thumbs and little paths of blood snaked quietly down between our fingers while the seals that had drifted down from distant Labrador wept and moaned like human children on the ice-floes of the Gulf.

In the daytime my mother's brother who had been my father's partner as long as I could remember also came to work upon the gear. He was a year older than my mother and was tall and dark and the father of twelve children.

By March we were very far behind and although I began to work very hard in the evenings I knew it was not hard enough and that there were but eight weeks left before the opening of the season on May first. And I knew that my mother worried and my uncle was uneasy and that all of our very lives depended on the boat being ready with her gear and two men, by the date of May the first. And I knew then that *David Copperfield* and *The Tempest* and all of those friends I had dearly come to love must really go forever. So I bade them all good-bye.

The night after my first full day at home and after my mother had gone upstairs he called me into his room where I sat upon the chair beside his bed. "You will go back tomorrow," he said simply.

I refused then, saying I had made my decision and was satisfied.

"That is no way to make a decision," he said, "and if you are satisfied I am not. It is best that you go back." I was almost angry then and told him as all children do that I wished he would leave me alone and stop telling me what to do.

He looked at me a long time then, lying there on the same bed on which he had fathered me those sixteen years before, fathered me his only son, out of who knew what emotions when he was already fifty-six and his hair had turned to snow. Then he swung his legs over the edge of the squeaking bed and sat facing me and looked into my own dark eyes with his of crystal blue and placed his hand upon my knee. "I am not telling you to do anything," he said softly, "only asking you."

The next morning I returned to school. As I left, my mother followed me to the porch and said, "I never thought a son of mine would choose useless books over the parents that gave him life."

In the weeks that followed he got up rather miraculously and the gear was ready and the *Jenny Lynn* was freshly painted by the last two weeks of April when the ice began to break up and the lonely screaming gulls returned to haunt the silver herring as they flashed within the sea.

On the first day of May the boats raced out as they had always done, laden down almost to the gunwales with their heavy cargoes of traps. They were almost like living things as they plunged through the waters of the spring and manoeuvred between the still floating icebergs of crystal-white and emerald green on their way to the traditional grounds that they sought out every May. And those of us who sat that day in the high school on the hill, discussing the water imagery of Tennyson, watched them as they passed back and forth beneath us until by afternoon the piles of traps which had been stacked upon the wharf were no longer visible but were spread about the bottoms of the sea. And the *Jenny Lynn* went too, all day, with my uncle tall and dark, like a latter-day Tashtego standing at the tiller with his legs wide apart and guiding her deftly between the floating pans of ice and my father in the stern standing in the same way with his hands upon the ropes that lashed the cargo to the deck. And at night my mother asked, "Well, how did things go in the boat today?"

And the spring wore on and the summer came and school ended in the third week of June and the lobster season on July first and I wished that the two things I loved so dearly did not exclude each other in a manner that was so blunt and too clear.

At the conclusion of the lobster season my uncle said he had been offered a berth on a deep sea dragger and had decided to accept. We all knew that he was leaving the *Jenny Lynn* forever and that before the next lobster season he would buy a boat of his own. He was expecting another child and would be supporting fifteen people by the next spring and could not chance my father against the family that he loved.

I joined my father then for the trawling season, and he made no protest and my mother was quite happy. Through the summer we baited the tubs of trawl in the afternoon and set them at sunset and revisited them in the darkness of the early morning. The men would come tramping by our house at four A.M. and we would join them and walk with them to the wharf and be on our way before the sun rose out of the ocean where it seemed to spend the night. If I was not up they would toss pebbles to my window and I would be very embarrassed and tumble downstairs to where my father lay fully clothed atop his bed, reading his book and listening to his radio and smoking his cigarette. When I appeared he would swing off his

bed and put on his boots and be instantly ready and then
we would take the lunches my mother had prepared the
night before and walk off toward the sea. He would make
no attempt to wake me himself.

It was in many ways a good summer. There were few
storms and we were out almost every day and we lost a
minimum of gear and seemed to land a maximum of fish
and I tanned dark and brown after the manner of my
uncles.

My father did not tan – he never tanned – because of his
reddish complexion, and the salt water irritated his skin as
it had for sixty years. He burned and reburned over and
over again and his lips still cracked so that they bled when
he smiled, and his arms, especially the left, still broke out
into the oozing salt-water boils as they had ever since as a
child I had first watched him soaking and bathing them in
a variety of ineffectual solutions. The chafe-preventing
bracelets of brass linked chain that all the men wore about
their wrists in early spring were his the full season and he
shaved but painfully and only once a week.

And I saw then, that summer, many things that I had
seen all my life as if for the first time and I thought that
perhaps my father had never been intended for a fisherman either physically or mentally. At least not in the
manner of my uncles; he had never really loved it. And I
remembered that, one evening in his room when we were
talking about *David Copperfield*, he had said that he had
always wanted to go to the university and I had dismissed
it then in the way one dismisses his father's saying he
would like to be a tight-rope walker, and we had gone on
to talk about the Peggottys and how they loved the sea.

And I thought then to myself that there were many
things wrong with all of us and all our lives and I wondered why my father, who was himself an only son, had
not married before he was forty and then I wondered why
he had. I even thought that perhaps he had had to marry
my mother and checked the dates on the flyleaf of the
Bible where I learned that my oldest sister had been born

a prosaic eleven months after the marriage, and I felt myself then very dirty and debased for my lack of faith and for what I had thought and done.

And then there came into my heart a very great love for my father and I thought it was very much braver to spend a life doing what you really do not want rather than selfishly following forever your own dreams and inclinations. And I knew then that I could never leave him alone to suffer the iron-tipped harpoons which my mother would forever hurl into his soul because he was a failure as a husband and a father who had retained none of his own. And I felt that I had been very small in a little secret place within me and that even the completion of high school was for me a silly shallow selfish dream.

So I told him one night very resolutely and very powerfully that I would remain with him as long as he lived and we would fish the sea together. And he made no protest but only smiled through the cigarette smoke that wreathed his bed and replied, "I hope you will remember what you've said."

The room was now so filled with books as to be almost Dickensian, but he would not allow my mother to move or change them and he continued to read them, sometimes two or three a night. They came with great regularity now, and there were more hard covers, sent by my sisters who had gone so long ago and now seemed so distant and so prosperous, and sent also pictures of small red-haired grandchildren with baseball bats and dolls which he placed upon his bureau and which my mother gazed at wistfully when she thought no one would see. Red-haired grandchildren with baseball bats and dolls who would never know the sea in hatred or in love.

And so we fished through the heat of August and into the cooler days of September when the water was so clear we could almost see the bottom and the white mists rose like delicate ghosts in the early morning dawn. And one day my mother said to me, "You have given added years to his life."

And we fished on into October when it began to roughen and we could no longer risk night sets but took our gear out each morning and returned at the first sign of the squalls; and on into November when we lost three tubs of trawl and the clear blue water turned to a sullen grey and the trochoidal waves rolled rough and high and washed across our bows and decks as we ran within their troughs. We wore heavy sweaters now and the awkward rubber slickers and the heavy woollen mitts which soaked and froze into masses of ice that hung from our wrists like the limbs of gigantic monsters until we thawed them against the exhaust pipe's heat. And almost every day we would leave for home before noon, driven by the blasts of the northwest wind, coating our eyebrows with ice and freezing our eyelids closed as we leaned into a visibility that was hardly there, charting our course from the compass and the sea, running with the waves and between them but never confronting their towering might.

And I stood at the tiller now, on these homeward lunges, stood in the place and in the manner of my uncle, turning to look at my father and to shout over the roar of the engine and the slop of the sea to where he stood in the stern, drenched and dripping with the snow and the salt and the spray and his bushy eyebrows caked in ice. But on November twenty-first, when it seemed we might be making the final run of the season, I turned and he was not there and I knew even in that instant that he would never be again.

On November twenty-first the waves of the grey Atlantic are very very high and the waters are very cold and there are no signposts on the surface of the sea. You cannot tell where you have been five minutes before and in the squalls of snow you cannot see. And it takes longer than you would believe to check a boat that has been running before a gale and turn her ever so carefully in a wide and stupid circle, with timbers creaking and straining, back into the face of storm. And you know that it is useless and that your voice does not carry the length of the boat and that even if you knew the original spot, the relentless waves would carry such a burden perhaps a mile or so by the time you could return. And you know also, the final irony, that your father like your uncles and all the men that form your past, cannot swim a stroke.

The lobster beds off the Cape Breton coast are still very rich and now, from May to July, their offerings are packed in crates of ice, and thundered by the gigantic transport trucks, day and night, through New Glasgow, Amherst, Saint John and Bangor and Portland and into Boston where they are tossed still living into boiling pots of water, their final home.

And though the prices are higher and the competition tighter, the grounds to which the *Jenny Lynn* once went remain untouched and unfished as they have for the last ten years. For if there are no signposts on the sea in storm there are certain ones in calm and the lobster bottoms were distributed in calm before any of us can remember and the grounds my father fished were those his father fished before him and there were others before and before and before. Twice the big boats have come from forty and fifty miles, lured by the promise of the grounds, and strewn the bottom with their traps and twice they have returned to find their buoys cut adrift and their gear lost and destroyed. Twice the Fisheries Officer and the Mounted Police have come and asked many long and involved questions and twice they have received no answers from the men leaning in the doors of their shanties and the women standing at their windows with their children in their arms. Twice they have gone away saying: "There are no legal boundaries in the Marine area"; "No one can own the sea"; "Those grounds don't wait for anyone."

But the men and the women, with my mother dark among them, do not care for what they say, for to them the grounds are sacred and they think they wait for me.

It is not an easy thing to know that your mother lives alone on an inadequate insurance policy and that she is too proud to accept any other aid. And that she looks through her lonely window onto the ice of winter and the hot flat calm of summer and the rolling waves of fall. And that she lies awake in the early morning's darkness when the rubber boots of the men scrunch upon the gravel as they pass beside her house on their way down to the wharf. And she knows that the footsteps never stop, because no man goes from her house, and she alone of all the Lynns has neither son nor son-in-law that walks toward the boat that will take him to the sea. And it is not an easy thing to know that your mother looks upon the sea with love and on you with bitterness because the one has been so constant and the other so untrue.

But neither is it easy to know that your father was found on November twenty-eighth, ten miles to the north and wedged between two boulders at the base of the rock-strewn cliffs where he had been hurled and slammed so many many times. His hands were shredded ribbons as were his feet which had lost their boots to the suction of the sea, and his shoulders came apart in our hands when we tried to move him from the rocks. And the fish had eaten his testicles and the gulls had pecked out his eyes and the white-green stubble of his whiskers had continued to grow in death, like the grass on graves, upon the purple, bloated mass that was his face. There was not much left of my father, physically, as he lay there with the brass chains on his wrists and the seaweed in his hair.

SEVEN

The Road to Rankin's Point

I AM speaking now of a July in the early 1970's and it is in the morning just after the sun has risen following a night of heavy rains. My car moves through the quiet village which is yet asleep except for those few houses which have sent fishermen to their nets and trawls some hours before. From such houses the smoke whisks and curls lazily before slanting off at the insistence of the almost imperceptible southeast wind. Upon my right the Gulf of St. Lawrence is flat and blue, dotted here and there with the white fishing boats intent on their quiet work. It has been a bad year for lobsters because of the late ice and then the early storms which destroyed so much of the precious gear. During the last week of the lobster season many of the fishermen did not even visit their traps, preferring to remain drunk and discouraged on the beach or within the dampened privacy of their little shanties.

Now since the lobster season's conclusion on July first, it can be at least thankfully forgotten along with the vague feelings of hope tinged with guilt that accompanied its final days. The boats presently riding on the Gulf are after a variety of "ground fish," with some few after salmon. They are getting six cents a pound for hake and twelve for cod and no one has seen a haddock for a long, long time. In the cities of Ontario fresh cod sells for $1.65 a pound and the "dried cod" upon which most of us were raised and so heartily despised has become almost a delicacy which sells for $2.15 a pound. "Imagine that," says my grandmother, "who would have ever thought?" Across Cabot Strait in Newfoundland the prices are three to four cents lower and there is talk that the fishermen may strike. All this runs through my mind now although it does not really occupy it. Like the vaguely heard melody of some tuned-down radio station heard softly in the background.

At the outskirts of the village the narrow paved road turns to the left, away from the sea, and begins its journey inland and outward. If followed relentlessly it will take you almost anywhere in North America; perhaps to Central and to South America as well. It will remain narrow and unpretentious and "slow" in the caution that it demands of its drivers for approximately fifty miles. Then it will join the maple-leafed Trans-Canada Highway and together they will boom across the Canso Causeway and off Cape Breton Island and out into the world. As the water of the tributary joins the major river, its traffic and its travellers will blend and mingle within the rushing stream. They will become the camper trailers with their owners' names emblazoned on their sides, and the lumbering high-domed motor homes and the over-crowded station wagons with the dogs forever panting through the rear windows. They will become the high-powered "luxury" products of Detroit, loaded with extras and zooming at eighty miles per hour from service station to service station, as if by speed alone they might some-how outrace the galloping depreciation which even now threatens to overtake and engulf them. They will become the scuttling Volkswagens in the "slow" lanes on the long hills and the grinding trucks with their encased and T-shirted drivers carrying the continent's goods and the weaving, swerving motorcyclists with their helmets reflecting the slanting sun.

By night these travellers will all be miles away; comparing mileages, filling their radiators and looking at their maps. They will be sitting around campfires and sweating in the motels. Some will be in the havens of their homes while others will follow the probing paths of their bugspattered headlights deep into the darkened night. Some few will end in the twisted, spectacular wreckages, later moaning incoherently in the unknown hospitals or lying beneath the quiet sheets of death while authorities search through glove compartments and check out licence numbers prior to notifying the next of kin. It is a big, fast, brutal road that leads into the world on this July day and there is no longer any St. Christopher to be the patron saint of travellers.

But for me, in this my twenty-sixth year, it is not into the larger world that I go today. And the road that I follow feeds into no other that will take the traveller to the great adventures of the wild unknown. Instead, at the village's end its veers sharply to the right, leaves the pavement behind and almost immediately begins to climb along the rocky cliffs that hang high above the sea. It winds its tortuous, clinging way for some eight miles before it ends quite abruptly and permanently in my grandmother's yard. There the sea cliff slants down almost vertically and it is as if the road runs into it as it would into a wall. At the wall's base and at the road's end nestles my grandmother's tiny farm; her buildings and her home. Above this last small cultivated outpost and jutting beyond it out to sea is the rocky promontory of Rankin's Point. As one cannot drive beyond it, neither can one see beyond it farther up the coast. It is an end in every way and it is to the beginning of this conclusion that my car now begins its long ascent.

For the first two miles there are still houses strung out along both sides of the road but soon such signs of formal habitation fall behind; and as the road becomes steeper, rockier and more narrow the wildness of the summer's beauty falls and splashes down upon it even to the extent that it is close to lost. The overreaching branches of the silver birch, the maple and the poplar slap across the hood and windshield impeding vision and almost the passage of the road itself. The alders lean and hang from the left bank, their sticky buds smearing the car door's sides and leaving stains that will annoy car washers for a long, long time. The wild flowers burst and hang in all their short-lived, giddy, aromatic profusion. When the tough but deli-cate red-and-white roses are nudged by the car they cas-cade and strew their fragile, perfumed petals across its hood even as their thorns scratch the finished lacquer of its sides. *Everything has its price*, they seem to say. The sweet red-and-white clover swarms with bees. The yellow buttercups flutter and the white and gold-green daisies dip and sway. The prickly Scottish thistles are in their laven-der bloom and the wild buckwheat and rioting raspberry bushes form netted tapestries of the darkest green. As the road dips and twists around many of its hairpinned turns the icy little streams cascade across it; washing it out in a minor way, the water flowing across the gullied roadbed instead of beneath it through the broken, plugged and unused wooden sluices. At such spots near the fresh water's edge the bluebells cling to the velvet-mossed stones and the blue-and-purple irises march downward to the wetness. The gentle, large-eyed rabbits hop trustingly near the road which is so untravelled that it holds for them neither fear nor any threat of death. The road is now but a minor intrusion that the wildness will reclaim.

Before the final two-mile climb there is one last almost right-angled turn and again the spilling, cascading brook and the washed-over roadbed and the plugged and useless sluice. The road rising from the spot is solid rock and on wet days it is impossible for a car to make the climb. The tires will spin and the rear of the car will slew to the right and hang above the four-hundred-foot drop that falls to the crashing surf which booms and pounds the smooth and rounded boulders far below. Three years ago a lovers' quarrel resulted in a car being stolen from the village below and then pushed over the towering cliff. For weeks the police and the insurance companies and various high-priced towing companies attempted to reach it but with no success. All of the cables and the extended booms and the huge tow trucks that were reared back on their hind and doubled wheels and the men motioning with their gloved hands or hanging on ropes at the sea cliff's wall did nothing to raise the twisted bits of metal that were scattered far below. Finally some men in a small fishing dory were able to get close enough to the cliff's base to wade ashore in water up to their waists and retrieve what remained of the engine. Now if one hangs over the perilous edge the remaining bits of automobile can still be seen strewn along the wet cliff's base. Here the twisted chassis and there the detached body and yards away the steering wheel and the trunk lid and a crumpled, twisted door. The cormorants and the gulls walk carefully amidst the twisted wreckage as if hoping that each day may bring them something that they had previously missed. They peck with curiosity at the gleaming silver knobs and the selector buttons of the once-expensive radio.

The sharp, right-angled turn and its ascending steepness has always been called by us "The Little Turn of Sadness" because it is here that my grandfather died so many years ago on a February night when he somehow fell as he walked or staggered toward his home which was a steep two miles away. He had already covered the six miles from the village when he lost his footing on the ice-covered rock, falling backwards and shattering the rum bottle he carried within his safe back pocket. Now as I feel my own blood, diseased and dying, I think of his, the brightest scarlet, staining the moon-white snow while the joyous rabbits leaped and pirouetted beneath the pale, clear moon. It was a bright and quiet night without a breath of wind, as my grandmother has often told us. All night she kept looking out across the death-white fields for the form of her returning husband. Her eyes became so strained that as the dawn approached the individual spruce trees at the clearing's edge began to take his shape and size and seemed to move toward the house. First one and then another appearing to move and take on human form.

Once she was so certain that she went to the door and opened it only to stare again across the whitened, empty stillness of the silent winter snow.

In the morning she sent her oldest son, who was ten at the time, to walk along the frozen cliffs; and when he returned, white and breathless, the news he brought was already expected. Shortly after he left, she has often said, she began to hear the death ring or the sound of the death bell in her right ear. It came from off the frozen Gulf of St. Lawrence borne on the stillness and, no, it was not to be confused with the crying of the white and drifting seals. And then almost in response to the bell she had heard the howls of the three black-and-white border collies that had accompanied her son. Their howls drifted back along the coastline, first the oldest dog and then the second and then the third. She had been able to distinguish each dog's cry and to comprehend the message that their anguished voices bore. At that time and in those sounds she realized that life for her and for her children would never be the same. She was twenty-six and expecting her seventh child.

Later she and her older children hitched the best of their brown-dappled horses to the wood sleigh and went forth to meet their husband and father for the final time. The children cried and the tears froze to their reddened cheeks. The horse began to snort and tremble long before he reached the rigid, log-like figure and then to rear and plunge. Finally he lunged to the side, breaking the shafts of the precious sleigh and adding another stick of destruction to the steadily mounting pile. They had had to abandon the sleigh then and return with the horse and then come back again with the children's coasting sleigh and lengths of rope with which to bind the grizzly burden it was to bear.

The dogs lay restlessly about the stiffened corpse, black against the silent snow. Sometimes they whined softly and licked the frozen opened eyes or the grotesquely parted purple lips with the protruding tongue or nuzzled an out-flung half-curved arm. Then they would flop back again into the snow, covering their noses with their paws while following everything with their deep brown eyes. Sensing too that their lives had changed and not knowing what to do.

Somehow they managed the final two miles though their own feet slipped on the icy rocks and they fell forward several times when the strained rope parted. Because the sleigh was so small there was only room for the upper part of the body, and the legs and heels hung over the end and dragged along the jagged, stony road. Twice it almost slipped off completely and when they reached the house the heels of the rubber boots were worn through to the frozen flesh. The heel of the bottle which had killed him still contained, almost miraculously, a half inch of the dark sweet rum while the neck with its firmly fastened cork was also still intact. Between the perfect top and the perfect bottom all was shattered and splintered and driven deeply into the frozen hip and thigh.

Now this scene of winter death seems strangely out of place amidst the drunken intensity of the summer's splendour. Like an improbable sequence of old black-and-white pictures taken once in the long ago. Taken of people it is impossible to ever know or to fully understand.

The sun is rising above the mountains and touching the freshly washed earth. The raindrops glisten and sparkle, and the fog and mists that hang above the dirt roads of high places rise and vanish toward the sky. The bobolinks and red-winged blackbirds bounce and sing from the tips of their springing willows. Orange butterflies glide and float on the drafts of air and the chattering squirrels and chipmunks sprint along the fallen logs like busy proprietors doing morning inspection. The earth is alive, refreshed and new.

It does not take long for the rocks above "The Little Turn of Sadness" to dry, and my car in its lowest gear grinds slowly and reluctantly up the steep incline, nearly swinging out and over the hanging ledge, then settling more steadily to the stony and almost familiar roadbed.

For the next two miles the road continues to climb and wind along the cliff's high ledge. In some places erosion has caused the roadside to crumble and fall into the sea. It would be impossible for two vehicles to meet and pass upon such narrowness but there is little likelihood of such an occurrence.

Now and then upon the left I see the remains of the old stone fences and also tiny patches of still cleared land indicating where houses had once stood. The grey granite stones of their foundations are still visible, covered now with green and velvet moss. Now and then a stone flue stands with phallic reality amidst the rubble of the house that has fallen down around it. Only the strength of stone has survived the ravages of time and seasons.

A mile from my grandmother's house her sheep begin to appear, grazing or lying along the roadside and sometimes right in the middle of the road. They are the white-faced Cheviots that she has had for as long as I can remember and there is almost a timelessness about them. Open faced and independent they do not flock together as do the more conventional Oxfords and Suffolks. As the car approaches, the young lambs bound and scramble out of its way bleating over their shoulders to the patient, watchful ewes. The thick-shouldered rams, with their heavy, swinging scrota almost dragging on the ground, move only at the last minute and then begrudgingly. Their flickering eyes seem to say they would as soon lower their heads and charge than relinquish this stony trail which they obviously consider to be theirs.

For decades my grandmother has been concerned about the purity and well-being of these sheep. She has worried about strange rams interbreeding and diluting her "stock." And she has worried about young dogs wild with spring and bloodlust running them over the cliffs to sea-washed deaths. Now there is no need to worry. All the other flocks and dogs from the fallen houses have gone and it is only her sheep whose bleating cries reverberate across these high cleansed hills.

At the road's end I stop to slide back the poles of the old gate before the final entrance to her yard. As I bend, the blood bursts from my nostrils, splashing scarletly upon my shoes, and there is a dizzying lightness bordering on black within my head. I straighten and place my hands on the gateposts for steadiness and lift my face to the sun to reverse the blood's thick flow. I can feel it coursing sweetly through the back of my mouth and down the darkened passages of my throat. To avoid further bending, I slide the bottom pole back by hooking my right foot underneath it and then stand and wait for the bleeding to cease. I dab at my nostrils and lips with the pieces of Kleenex that I now carry in place of standard handkerchiefs.

The car, with its clutch disengaged, rolls easily down the small incline into the yard. There is no need to even start the motor. I close the gate watched with interest by various farm animals who are not in the least alarmed. Almost all of my grandmother's animals are descended from livestock that has been here for a long, long time and over the years they have taken on distinctive colourings and characteristics that are all their own. They seem now the same animals that I have always known and heard described, and seen in the faded photographs of the albums of my mind. The three brown-dappled horses, rolling in the slickness of their summer fat, have an almost maroon tinge to their coats when the sun strikes them at certain angles. They have identical white stars in their foreheads and a solitary white spot the size of a large coin on their barrelled chests. They have always been called either Star or Tena. They have always held their heads high when drawing even the heaviest of loads and have been perfectly in step with each other, their hoofbeats falling in unison through the regulated choreography of their fiercely inbred generations. They have been sure-footed in the snow and long-winded on the hills. They have crossed the drift ice in the blinding blizzards and galloped the cartloads of seaweed ashore across the briny rocks. For years they have refused to eat any hay except that grown upon this hilly farm; as if smelling and tasting within it their own urine, manure and sweat. As if they are part of some great ecological plan, converting themselves into hay and the hay in turn into their wine-dappled sun-strong selves.

Now standing about this yard, whisking their too-long tails and tossing their forelocks out of their eyes, they are idle and at ease. They have felt neither bridle nor harness nor shoes for years and the youngest who is close to ten has never felt them at all. He is so old now, in the years of a horse, that it is unlikely that he ever will.

They have become almost pets waiting for my grandmother to open her door and offer them bits of apple or pieces of stale, dried bread. Yet in their deep, dark eyes and in the muscles that bunch and ripple within their shoulders their power can still be seen. They are like the eyes and muscles of certain animals at the zoo; eyes and muscles that say, *Yes, we are here and we are alive and we eat our food, but we were not bred for this kind of life nor did we come from it nor is this all we are. Look closely at us and you will see.*

The brindled cows with their in-curved horns are busily grazing about the grassy knolls. Because my grandmother no longer tends them as she used to, nor uses their cream-rich milk for her butter and cheese, they too seem wasted and unused. They are followed by overgrown calves who nurse and butt at their swollen and distended udders. Some of their udders are caked and hardened and mastitis has set in. It would be close to impossible to redeem them now and they will nevermore fill to overflow the warm and brimming pails. A black hen with gold flecks around her neck is clucking to her chickens. The chickens are too young for this time of year and will not likely survive the fall.

Entering the porch that leads to my grandmother's house it is necessary to step down. With the passage of the years the house has sunk into the earth. The stone foundation of more than a century has worked itself deep into the soil and now all doors are forced to open inward. The porch is filled with tools and clothes and items from the past. A manual cream separator is on the left, a hand scythe hangs on the wall to the right, and beside it a wire stretcher and a meat grinder. Bits of harness and rope and cans of fence staples, nails, hammers, gunny sacks and fishing rods hang from the spikes driven deep into the wooden beams. Shapeless rain jackets, hats, gloves, and worn-out shoes and boots hang and lie cluttered in a corner.

In the kitchen my grandmother sits at her table drinking her morning tea. She has not seen nor heard my arrival and she is staring out the window that looks upon the sea. There the gulls are curving and turning in the sparkling sun. The three black-and-white border collies raise their eyes when I enter but they do not move. They lie about the floor like tossed and familiar rugs. One is under the table, one against the wood box at the stove, and the third beside my grandmother's chair. Unlike my grandmother, they have been aware of my approach for some time. They have recognized the sound of the motor groaning along the cliff's edge and heard the gate poles slide and the opening of the door and the footstep on the sill. They have heard it all and felt no cause for movement or alarm. I enter now to make my presence fully known and to take my place in time.

Turning from the window with her teacup in her hand, my grandmother is startled to see me and also embarrassed that I have come upon her so silently and unannounced. She is becoming frightened, although she will not admit it, of the loss of her senses, and she fears the silence of the deaf and the darkness of the blind. None of this has happened to her as yet but there are clutching moments seen in her face, as now, that say such thoughts are there.

"Oh, you are here, Calum," she says. "I've been expecting you."

I know that she has as I have been expecting to come,

lying in the bed at my parents' house in the village below since three A.M., listening to the rain upon the roof and thinking of how slippery the rocks of the road might be. Thinking of walking the eight-mile distance in the almost unfathomable rural darkness when the rain clouds blot out the moon and stars and there is only the sound of water: the thunking of the large-dropped rain into the earth and into the splashing, invisible brooks and on the right the lapping and moaning of the sea. Knowing that I will never walk that skin-drenched journey again, any more than will my never-seen grandfather, dead now for seventy years, the biblical life span of three score years and ten.

"I came as soon as I could," I say. "As soon as I thought the cliff would be dry enough for the car to climb."

"Oh yes," she says. "Would you like some tea? The kettle has just finished boiling."

"Yes, all right, I will get it myself," I say as I move about her familiar kitchen, digging into the old square tea can which drifted ashore from one of the long-ago wrecked vessels carrying the precious cargo from Ceylon. I gather the tea into my fist and drop it into the teapot and add the water from the steaming kettle.

"They will not be here for a while," she says, "not likely until the afternoon."

She seats herself more comfortably at the end of the table.

"Get yourself some biscuits from out of the tin. I made them early this morning. Give some to the dogs."

Obediently I go to another tin and take out four biscuits. They are still warm to the touch. I butter one for myself and toss one to each of the lying, watchful dogs. They catch them while they are still in the air, then flick out their long, pink tongues for any crumbs that may have fallen on the floor. The floor remains as spotless as before, as if the action had never happened. Like footsteps in the water, I think. No trace remains behind.

I sit opposite my grandmother at the other end of the

table and look with her out across the azure sea. The sun is higher now and the mists have all burned off. It is the kind of day that at one time would have allowed us to see Prince Edward Island. *On a clear day you can see Prince Edward Island*, we would say. Not "forever," just Prince Edward Island. Now it does not seem to matter.

Today is the first day of the rest of your life, comes to my mind. The slogan from the many "modern" posters, desk mottoes, greeting cards, book marks, record jackets, bumper stickers, and graffiti walls. I raise the teacup to my lips, half hopeful it might burn me more fiercely into life.

"Why do you drink your tea like that?" asks my grandmother. "You will burn yourself. One would think you had never drunk tea before."

"It is all right," I say. "I was only trying something."

We sit for a long time, quietly sipping our tea and looking through the window. We do not say what is on our minds nor make inquiries of each other. We are resting and appearing normal, almost as athletes quietly conserving our energy for the game that lies some hours down our road. The bees buzz from the lilacs at the base of the house and bounce drunkenly against the window. The barn swallows with their delicately forked tails flash their orange breasts and dart and swoop after invisible insects. The dogs lie silently, moving only their eyes, conserving their strength as well. We are drowsy and waiting in the summer's heat.

I have come to see my grandmother on this day almost as the double agent of the spy movies. I have come somehow hoping that I might find a way of understanding and of coming to terms with death; yet deep down I know that I will find only the intensity of life and that I am, after all, but twenty-six, and in the eyes of others, in the youngness of my years.

My grandmother gets up and goes for her violin which hangs on a peg inside her bedroom door. It is a very old violin and came from the Scotland of her ancestors, from the crumbled foundations that now dot and haunt

Lochaber's shores. She plays two Gaelic airs – *Gun Bhris Mo Chridh' On Dh 'Fhalbh Thu* (My Heart Is Broken Since Thy Departure) and *Cha Till Mi Tuille* (Never More Shall I Return or MacCrimmon's Lament). Her hands have suffered stiffness and the lonely laments waver and hesitate as do the trembling fingers upon the four taut strings. She is very moved by the ancient music and there are tears within her eyes.

On the night of this day and on this afternoon as well, two of her grandchildren and one great-grandchild will gyrate and play the music of their time; the music of the early 1970's. They are at other destinations on that other road that leads into the larger world. One is in Las Vegas and two on Toronto's Yonge Street strip. They swivel and stomp beneath kaleidoscopic lights, stepping nimbly over the cords that bind their instruments to the high-powered amplifiers. Their long hair floats and swirls about their shoulders and their hard-driving booted heels are as insistent as their rhythms. Here in the quietness of Rankin's Point, at another road's end, the body out of which they came and to which they owe their lives has trouble controlling the last quavering notes of Never More Shall I Return.

"That is the lament of the MacCrimmons," she says when she has finished. "Your grandfather was part MacCrimmon. They were the greatest musicians in the Scottish Highlands. There is a cairn erected to their memory on the Isle of Skye. Your uncles saw it during the war."

"Yes, I know," I say. "You've told me."

"The MacCrimmons were said to be given two gifts," she says, "the gift of music and the gift of foreseeing their own deaths. Those gifts are supposed to follow in all their bloodlines. They are not gifts of the ordinary world."

High on the rafters of the barn that stands outside, my grandfather had written in the blackest of ink the following statement: "We are the children of our own despair, of Skye and Rum and Barra and Tiree." No one knows why he wrote it or when, and even the "how" gives cause for puzzlement. In that time before ballpoint pens or even fountain pens, did he climb such heights holding an ink bottle in one hand and a straight nibbed pen in the other? And what is the significance of ancestral islands long left and never seen? Blown over now by Atlantic winds and touched by scudding foam. What does it mean to all of us that he died as he did? And had he not, how would our grandmother's life have been different and the lives of her children and even mine as I have known it and still feel it as I sit here on this day?

I can know my grandfather only through recreated images of his life and death. Images of the frozen snow and the hot blood turned to crust upon it; blood, hot and sweet with rum and instantly converted like the sweet and boiling maple sap upon the winter's snow.

I would like to realize and understand now my grand-mother's perception of death in all its vast diversity. For even the fixedness of death and the accidents that are its agents have changed throughout the years of her many-sequenced life. Three of her brothers, as young men, per-ished in the accidental ways that grew out of their lives – lives that were as intensely physical as the deaths that marked their end. One as a young man in the summer sun when the brown-dappled horses bolted and he fell into the teeth of a mowing machine. A second in a storm at sea when the vessel sank while plying its way across the straits to Newfoundland. A third frozen upon the lunar ice fields of early March when the sealing ship became separated from its men in a sudden obliterating blizzard.

How lonely now and distant these lives and deaths of my grandmother's early life. And how different from the lives and deaths of the three sons she has outlived. Men who left the crying gulls and hanging cliffs of Rankin's Point to take the road into the larger world and there to fashion careers and lives that would never have been theirs on this tiny sea-washed farm. Careers that were as modern and as affluent as the deaths that marked their termination. Real estate brokers and vice-presidents of grocery chains and buyers for haberdashery firms seldom die in the daily routines of the working lives that they have chosen. The pencil and the telephone replace the broken, dangling reins and the marlinespike and the sealing club; and the adjusted thermostats and the methodic Muzak produce a regulated urban order far removed from the uncertainty of the elements and the unpredictability of suddenly frightened animals.

None of these men died at their work or directly from it, yet die they did in deaths that seem even more bizarre and Grecianly ironic than those of the previous generation. One of them choked on a piece of steak in an expensive Montreal restaurant. A second died at Pompano Beach from too much of the sun he had gone to find. The third died while jogging through the streets of Mississauga at five A.M.. Yet perhaps death by affluence is but the same in the end as that achieved through physical labour and perhaps it is only because I now have no choice of either that first one and then the other seems desperately more frightening.

Outside the window the blackbirds and cowbirds hop with familiarity around the brindle cows. They call out their raucous comments to one another and sometimes perch boldly upon the cattle's spines. A single, white-tailed hawk glides silently back and forth, sometimes above the land and then beyond the cliff's edge out toward the sea. His shadow slides beneath him across the summer grass but is not reflected within the deep, blue water. It is as if the mirror were perhaps too profound. He does not go far out to sea but circles and climbs and returns across the land; silent and graceful, holding his wings with rigid and controlled beauty, he bears with eloquence the message of his gifted life.

Within the house all is silent except for the ticking of the white Westclox on its shelf above the table. The dogs drowse with half-closed eyes. Lost within our own thoughts, we stay, as in a picture, quiet and immobile for a long, long time.

"Well, I suppose I must get ready. They will soon be here," says my grandmother, rising from her seat at the end of the table and seeming to break the spell.

Within her bedroom which opens off the kitchen, I can see or sense the combing of her long, white hair. She leans to one side and combs it away from her body, her left hand running along its electric smoothness ahead and behind of the comb she wields with her right.

Later she emerges, fastening a broach of entwined Scottish thistles to the collar of her recently ironed dress. I recognize both the broach and the dress as gifts that I have purchased for her at earlier times. For an instant I see myself once more in the press of pre-Christmas shoppers in Toronto, jostling and elbowing, moving on and off the crowded elevators and the humming, slanting escalators that stretch between the floors.

I know that in her trunks and scattered jewel boxes there are layers of dresses and mounds of broaches as good as these; yet she has chosen what she has quite consciously. Few of the others, I realize, will recognize what she wears, and there is of course no reason that they should. I am struck once more by the falseness of the broach, for Scottish thistles do not twine. Perhaps at the time of its purchase I was being more symbolic than I had ever thought.

Returning to her bedroom she emerges once more with a pair of scissors and draws her chair up close to mine. Without saying anything I begin to trim her fingernails. They are long and yellowed and each is bordered by a thin layer of grime.

Trimming the yellowed, unclean fingernails of my grandmother I realize that I am admitted now to the silent, secret communication that the strong have always known in their relationship with the weak. It is the strength and knowledge that my grandmother has previously so fiercely exercised over her own children and in many cases her children's children as well. The strength and knowledge leading into and from the awful privacy of all our secret inadequacies which is the standard that the previous generation waves always over the one that follows. The awareness and memory of dirty diapers and bed wettings and the first attempts at speech and movement; of the birth and death of Santa Claus and of the myriad childish hopes and fears of the lost time; of the lonely screaming nightmares of childhood terror; of nocturnal emissions and of real and imagined secret sins. The strength and knowledge of actual physical support and the giving and sustaining of such physical life and perhaps even love. I have never thought of my grandmother so much in terms of love as in terms of strength. Perhaps, I think now, because the latter has always been so much more visible.

Down in the village at this time I imagine my own father, now nearing seventy, preparing for his journey here to meet us. Nervously brushing his snow-white hair and slapping his face with talcum powder, still half afraid of his mother's inspection, bound too by those complex cords of strength and knowledge. He cannot, of course, remember ever seeing the father that was his own.

Suddenly my grandmother seizes my right hand and presses it fiercely between both of hers. The scissors that I have held clatter to the floor and I can feel the intensity of her life yearning and pressing outward through the pressure of her palms. "Oh, Calum," she says, "what are you going to do with the rest of your life?"

I do not know whether I am more shocked by the unexpectedness of the question or by what seems to be its enormity, given the circumstances. The doctor has said that I should try to live "the rest of my life" in as normal a fashion as possible. I have, he has said, "perhaps some months," in which I may continue to live and to appear as normal. I am reminded of the summer chickens outside my grandmother's door, doomed by their time of life to not survive the fall.

"Oh stay with me, Calum," she says, "and I will tell them so when they come. Find yourself a nice girl and get married. You are twenty-six and it is time to be thinking of such things. You have always liked it here and the land and the animals are as good as ever. You can make a good life here for all of us. I have left you everything in my will."

Outside the window I see the piles of roughened field stones picked by the strong, worn fingers of my grandmother's hands in earlier times. I see the falling rail fences and the outbuildings in need of paint and shingles. And the barn that contains my grandfather's only message. This is the "everything" left to me, I am told, by my grandmother's will. Yet no one has ever given me "everything" before and it is true that I have always liked it here amidst the loneliness and the privacy and the crying gulls. And I have thought of it many times during my "absent" years spent teaching the over-urbanized high school students of Burlington and Don Mills in the classrooms that always seemed so overheated. I have returned now, I think, almost as the diseased and polluted salmon, to swim for a brief time in the clear waters of my earlier stream. The returning salmon knows of no "cure" for the termination of his life.

I feel the blackened dizziness as it swirls within my head and clutch the chair's seat for support.

"What is the matter with you?" asks my grandmother. "You look like you are going to faint. Do you want a drink of water?"

"No," I say. "It will soon pass. It will soon be over."

The dogs, as if in concert, lift their heads and cock their ears and rise from their recumbent positions to move toward the door. They have heard the cars grinding along the cliff's edge some miles away. Neither my grandmother nor I can hear anything but we know that we are seeing the coming of sound to finer ears than ours. It is almost as if we can see the sound itself through an exchanging of the senses. Sometimes by looking at the face of the person on the telephone, you can see the nature of the news that is received although your ears hear only the silence that is no sound at all.

"They are coming," says my grandmother, giving a final pat to her hair.

The distant procession consists of members of her family and they are bound on an expedition which might best be entitled "What to do about Grandma?" It is an expedition which has set out with various degrees of optimism for the past fifteen years or so and it has always been launched in the summer when the maximum forces are available. In the summer, numbers of my grandmother's children and grandchildren and great-grandchildren and even great-great-grandchildren return from their scattered destinations on the roads of the larger world. Joining forces with the relatives who are residents of the region, they map and plan strategies which they hope will suit their purpose. Each year in the face of pleas and tears and petitions and almost threats, my grandmother has remained firm in her refusal to be moved from this her home. I see her quietly gathering her inner resources now, preparing her front of strength almost as if she is checking out her equipment. Images of old Cecil B. DeMille spectaculars come to mind, those pictures in which the attackers are repulsed from their desired heights by having boulders rolled down upon them or balls of flaming fire; sometimes they feel their scaling ladders tipped backwards so that they fall with screams and outstretched limbs. And yet our sympathy seems never to lie with them but instead with those who are besieged.

This year's strategy involves the nursing home in the village below and it is planned as an alternative to last year's failure which was called "living with us" and which was put forth by different people who varied greatly in their enthusiasm and reluctance. The advantages of the nursing home are "privacy" and "being with people near her own age" and "not having to worry about her meals" and receiving what is vaguely described as "care." There are various other "advantages" of the same type. On and on.

My grandmother has visited the nursing home at different times to see certain people who are her friends and she has hated it as much as do the friends she goes to see. Clutching her fingers in parchment hands they whisper to her in Gaelic which most of the staff can no longer understand. They tell her of real and imagined atrocities: that when the visitors leave the staff steal the Kleenex and the chocolates, that poison is being put in the food, that they are strapped to armchairs and wheelchairs for a long time, sitting in their own excrement and urine until their heads flop over onto their shoulders. What does it mean that old women in nursing homes suffer from real and imagined atrocities? And are the imagined ones less terrifying because they are not true?

Perhaps all of us, if we think of it, can see ourselves at some future time unable to use the bedpan in some place called Sunny Brae or Sunny Brook or Sunny Acres or Sunshine Villa; listening while the nurses' aides chew gum and talk about their dates (also real and imagined), "Oh he didn't" "Did he?" "You've got to be kidding!" Having our bodies hosed down by people who know too much about bodies and what they do or fail to do and how they finally end. This now I know is bearing down on me. It is ironically too distant and too close.

Once more I am concerned with my falseness and my cowardice. For I have been sent here on this day even as I have come of my own volition. I have been sent to make the initial request of my grandmother. "Perhaps she will go if Calum asks her," they have said. "If anyone can convince her it will be Calum." But Calum has done nothing but sit here all this morning. He has done nothing because he does not believe in this year's strategy any more than he did in that of the previous year. And in a secret place within his heart he hopes that it will fail.

Now as the cars begin to appear before the pole gate, I see myself as the failed advance rider sent out to scout the territory for the war party that is to follow. Or as an upside-down St. John the Baptist sent to prepare a false way for unlikely prophets. Or as the anguished and befuddled Judas already too close to his halter. At least I will not have to kiss her on the cheek.

After the cars have rolled into the yard, the people spill from them in all their vast variety. I stand at the door as an uncertain welcoming committee of one while my grandmother sits inside as she always does on such occasions. They are almost as a group of brightly coloured summer birds, these members of my family, chatting and laughing in plaid pants (with and without cuffs) and floral tops and sport shirts. Slacks, flares, denims, sandals and various "looks" that come from the variety of the worlds they inhabit and the ages that they are going through. Vaguely I think that they do not look much like people who are supposed to have the "gift" of foreseeing their own deaths.

They move into the house, smiling at me and patting me on the shoulder, some of them looking hopefully into my eyes for any message that might be found. Within the house which has not enough chairs, they arrange themselves as best they can, the children sitting on the floor with their arms around their knees. Soon they will run outside to play or be frightened by the animals that are so alien to many of them but for the present they must sit quietly because it is "polite."

Soon they begin to take the pictures. "Here is one of three generations," they say. "And now one of you and Mary and the baby. Four generations." Dutifully my grandmother holds her latest great-grandchild on her lap while her son and his daughter stand on either side of her. The people appear frozen as they look into the camera's lens.

Once as a boy in the summer following the last year of high school, my first cousin and I worked with my uncle on a ship taking barrels of salt fish to the islands of the West Indies and bringing back puncheons of dark and illegal rum. Upon our return we would anchor off the village in the still summer nights while the small local fishing boats plied diligently back and forth without lights and with muffled engines, landing the puncheons on the sandy beaches for the men who waited for them in the darkened pickup trucks.

Once, in Jamaica, my cousin and I were stopped on a street by a boy our own age who showed us a card and asked us to follow him. He took us to a brothel which was so unlike anything we had ever seen that we were actually afraid. When we finally convinced him we did not want "fun" he ushered us into the "picture room" which was only slightly less spectacular. Beautiful girls of all colours and races were being photographed in erotic poses with frightened young men who were about our own age. They undressed the young men and twined their hair about their genitals and brushed their penises with their lips. An energetic little dark-skinned man raced from one posing couple to the next, wheeling a bulky camera before him, shouting directions and asking the first names of the young men. Periodically he would disappear behind a curtain and emerge with the pictures. Across the front of each picture the same hand had written almost identical messages: "To John, my one and only love, Zelda." "To Tim, my one and only love, Tanya." "To George, my one and only love, Goldie."

"Coast Guard, mon!" said our acquaintance. Later we learned that the frightened and virginal-looking young men were members of a group of naval cadets from a Florida-based ship. They would keep the pictures in their wallets and show them secretly to their future friends, saying something like, "That's my girlfriend back home," and wait for the appreciative wows.

I think now that the photographs being taken here today share that same artificiality. In the family groupings in which people are relentlessly encouraged to smile, one cannot always see the desperate hopes and fears that flutter behind the eyes, or fully reach the darkest truth.

Glancing through the window I see my grandmother's

maroon-coloured horses and darkly brindled cattle moving about the automobiles that seem to fill the yard. Some of the automobiles bear the names of animals: Mustang, Pinto, Maverick. Soon children will have to be dispatched so that the real animals will not scratch or mar their metallized near namesakes.

As the afternoon moves on, the conversation rises and falls. People take flasks of rum from their pockets and pour drinks. My father and my uncles and aunts take the violin from its peg and play the complicated jigs and reels gracefully and without effort. All of them grasp the bow in the same spot and in the same manner and bend their wrists in an identical way. It is a style older than any of our memories and produces what we call "our sound." People remove harmonicas from handbags and pockets and the younger ones bring in guitars. Others rattle the kitchen spoons between their fingers and upon their thighs. My grandmother dances with each of her sons and then with the other men. She swings lightly and easily within my arms. There is no one in the nursing home who has lived as long as she.

The afternoon grows heightened and more animated while the question hovers like a whining, buzzing insect at the backs of all our minds. No one dares ask it and yet we are afraid to leave. From time to time people look hopefully toward me, raising their eyebrows, looking for a sign. My grandmother continues to dance and swing with easy grace. She is getting through her day. *If I can only hang on for another little while*, her eyes seem to say, *I can win this. I will not be defeated.* I think of her at twenty-six, pregnant and surrounded by weeping children, pulling home the frozen corpse of her husband on a children's sleigh. Perhaps saying the same thing. I cannot fathom how many times she must have said it in the seventy years between.

Too well I know all of the reasons put forth against her staying here. That it is lonely and isolated. That the house is old and heated only by stoves and illuminated but dimly by kerosene lamps. That there is no telephone. That in the winter members of her family must bring up her few groceries on snowmobiles when they can get through and that they are uncertain of what they then might find. That the animals are awkward and expensive and that she might fall and stumble while moving about them within their winter barns.

But I know also, as do most of us here, those other aspects of her life. Her dislike of institutions and her scorn of the "ease" associated with them. After her husband's death it was suggested by "authorities" from Halifax that she could never survive here and that it would "be better for everyone" if she were to move or put some of her children up for adoption or even in an orphanage. It would be "easier," they said. All of us here in this over-crowded room in the early 1970's with our rum and with our music are in some ways the result of her contradiction of such suggestions. Seventy years later. "I would never have my children taken from me to be scattered about like the down of a dead thistle," she has often said. "I would not be that dead. It does not matter that some things are difficult. No one has ever said that life is to be easy. Only that it is to be lived." I have come today, partially at least, hoping to find such strength for the living of my life and the meeting of my death.

The music stops and the sun moves westward. Younger children begin to whisper in their parents' ears that they are hungry and that they would like to leave. The tension seems to mount and crackle. We are waiting for the lightning that will provide us with release; looking at the balancing stone and waiting for its fall.

Suddenly and unexpectedly my grandmother says, "I hope none of you are worrying about me. Calum has said that he is going to stay here with me and now everything will be just fine."

There is a period of unbelieved silence followed by a great gush of relief. As if the plug of a bathtub or the valve of a tire has suddenly set free the contents that had been so controlled and well contained. People look at one another and at me in stunned amazement. The solution seems so perfect that it is almost impossible to comprehend. Much too good really to be true. My parents look at me in wonder that is mingled with relief. They have been uncertain concerning my unexpected return here from Ontario with what seems like no thought of ever going back. "Perhaps he will teach in the high school here," I have heard them say to one another. "Perhaps he is tired and needs a rest." I have not told them or anyone else that I have returned because I know I am to die and do not know where else to do it.

Now it seems that their questions have been temporarily answered and they are glad to know that I have had some plan during the days of this past time. They nod their heads and smile across the room, though still in wonder. My grandmother smiles as if she has just played her great trump card and looks about her in temporary triumph. I have not the courage to destroy the lie she so wishes to be true.

Almost immediately there is a great movement toward departure. It is as if they are afraid that their unexpected and magical gift might suddenly vanish should they stay too long within its presence. "Good-bye for now," they say. "See you later." "So long." "Take care."

The car doors slam, the motors start and the tires turn. The poles of the gate are slid back and then replaced by my father who is the last to leave. He waves to my grandmother and to me as we remain standing in the doorway. He is the middle link of our three generations. Then he too gets into his car beside my mother and drives away. We are left all alone.

Going back into the kitchen my grandmother busies herself in setting out the supper dishes. She takes the plates from the shelves and the knives and forks from the sliding drawers. The dogs who have been outside for most of the afternoon now return to flop upon the floor and resume their roles of quiet watchfulness. The sun is moving toward the sea.

"It is no good, Grandma," I say finally. "It is not going to work."

"What?" she says, keeping her back to me and reaching for the cups and saucers.

"What you told them. That I will stay here. It is not going to work." For a moment I teeter in hesitation but it seems that now I must go on. "It is not going to work," I say, "because I am going to die."

She turns and looks at me sharply and there is a flicker of fear upon her face which she banishes quickly. "Yes, I know," she laughs. "We all are. Sometime."

"It is no longer sometime," I say. "It is very soon. Only months. I am not going to see another spring. I will be of no use to you here nor any to myself. The doctors have said so."

"Don't be silly," she says. "You are only twenty-six. Your life is just beginning."

She looks at me with almost an indulgent tolerance for the silliness of my ideas and for my distortion of reality. Like the fond mother who is told by her imaginative child that he has seen a giraffe and an elephant upstairs in his bedroom. *I feel great affection for you*, the look says, *even though you do not know what you are talking about*.

For an instant I wish that it were so. To be as silly as she thinks I am and to be back in the time when bruises could be washed away by kisses and for her to be right and me thankfully wrong.

"No," I say. "It is true. Really true."

"What do you mean?" she asks, and now the true note of fear begins to sound in her voice. I wonder if it matches my own.

We sit at opposite ends of the kitchen table and look across at each other, across what seems the vast difference of our separated years. We make some attempts at conversation but they are not very successful.

Suddenly my grandmother leans across the table and

grasps my hand in hers. "Oh Calum, Calum," she says. "What are we going to do? What are we going to do? What is to become of us?"

The gesture is almost a replica of the one from the earlier afternoon. In looking at her hands I notice that I have never finished trimming her fingernails. I do not know what to say. She holds my hand so fiercely as if I might pull her from the dark waters of a dream. I try to respond to the pressure with my own hands for I too had somehow hoped I might be saved. Suddenly both of us burst into tears. We are weeping for each other and for ourselves. We two who had hoped to find strength in each other meet now instead in only this display of weeping weakness. The dogs cock their ears and whine softly. Moving from one of us to the other they rest their trusting heads upon our laps and look into our eyes.

Sometimes in the darkness of our fear it is difficult to distinguish the dream from the truth. Sometimes we wake from the dream beyond the midnight hour and it is so much better than the world to which we wake that we would will ourselves back into its soothing comfort. Sometimes the reverse is true and we would pinch ourselves or scrape our knuckles against the bed frame's steel. Sometimes the nightmare knows no lines.

Lying rigid now in this bed of my parents' house all the images and emotions of the past day meet and swirl in the outer and inner darkness. The hopes and fears of my past and present jostle and intertwine. Sometimes when seeing the end of our present our past looms ever larger because it is all we have or think we know. I feel myself falling back into the past now, hoping to have more and more past as I have less and less future. My twenty-six years are not enough and I would want to go farther and farther back through previous generations so that I might have more of what now seems so little. I would go back through the superstitions and the herbal remedies and the fatalistic war cries and the haunting violins and the cancer cures of cobwebs. Back through the knowledge of being and its end as understood through second sight and spectral visions and the intuitive dog and the sea bird's cry. I would go back to the priest with the magic hands. Back to the faith healer if only I had more faith. Back to anything rather than to die at the objective hands of mute, cold science.

I see that old but young MacCrimmon quietly composing the music of his own death before leaving permanently the darkened shores of his misty Skye. I hear the music now and it is almost like a bell even as I see him falling silently through the dark. How strange, I think, that anyone should even consider a violin as sounding like a bell.

I get up from my bed and put on my clothes and walk silently and carefully through the sleeping house. Outside it is very quiet. There is no industry in this region and late at night the silence is profound. The music seems to come from the ocean, from off the quiet Gulf, and, no, it is not to be confused with anything else. It is not a bird or a radio or a shunting train or a passing car. It is not coming from anyone's party. It is only itself, strangely familiar in its unfamiliar way.

And then almost in response to the bell I hear the howls of the three black-and-white border collies. They come borne on the night's stillness drifting along the lonely coastline that leads from Rankin's Point. First the oldest dog and then the second and then the third. I can distinguish each dog's cry and I can comprehend the message that their anguished voices bear. I will not be able to save my grandmother now, I know, any more than I was able to save her in the earlier afternoon.

My car follows its probing headlights up and down and around the hairpinned darkness of the road to Rankin's Point. Some of the turns are so extreme that it is easy to overdrive the headlights. Sometimes the lights shine straight ahead into the darkness of the green foliage even as the road cuts unexpectedly to the right or to the left and becomes at least temporarily invisible. I follow it easily as if guided through a dream.

At "The Little Turn of Sadness" my headlights pick up the eyes of the waiting dogs. They are lying in different positions in the middle of the road and their eyes glow out of the darkness like the highlighted points of a waiting triangle. Red and gleaming they serve as markers and as warnings; somewhat, I think, like the signal buoys of the harbour or the lights along an airstrip's edge.

When I leave the car they are glad to see me. *He will know what to do*, they seem to say. They are dogs who for centuries have been bred for the guiding and guarding of life. They are not the guardians of junkyards or used-car lots or closed-down supermarkets. Not the guardians of steel and stone but of lives as fragile and as uncertain as their own. Running silently to protect the sheep from the crumbling cliff or crouched beside the lamb with the broken leg, they have always worked closely with their human masters and have waited for them when faced with problems beyond their strength. Now they are glad that I have come and move toward me.

My grandmother lies in the middle of the road at the spot where the little brook washes over the roadbed before the steepness of the final climb. I kneel beside her and take her hands into mine. They are still warm to the touch and the fingernails are still untrimmed. No need for that now. There are no marks visible upon her body and her eyes are open and stare upwards into the darkness of the sky. The twining Scottish thistles are still pinned to the collar of her dress. This is the ending that we have.

I rise and climb the steep road until I am standing at the cliff's edge which faces out to sea. I turn my head to the left and try to look up the coast to the home and buildings of Rankin's Point, but I cannot see in the darkness. For the first time in the centuries since the Scottish emigrations there is no human life at the end of this dark road. I turn again to the open sea and concentrate very hard on seeing something but it is no use. My grandmother cannot see Prince Edward Island now nor ever will again. I look down into the darkness beneath my feet but there too there is only a darkened void although I can hear the water lapping gently on the boulders far below.

The music that my grandmother played in the long-ago morning of this day moves slowly through my mind. I cannot tell if it comes from without or from within and then it does not seem to matter. The darkness rises within me in dizzying swirls and seems to yearn for that other darkness that lies without. I reach for the steadying gate post or the chair's firm seat but there is nothing for the hand to touch. And then as with the music, the internal and the external darkness reach to become as one. Flowing toward one another they become enjoined and indistinct and as single as perfection. Without a seam, without a sound, they meet and unite all.

Afterword

BY JOYCE CAROL OATES

Since its publication in 1976, Alistair MacLeod's *The Lost Salt Gift of Blood* has become a Canadian classic. These lovingly and fastidiously crafted short stories are set in Cape Breton, an area of Canada remote to many Canadians though with a reputation of being a Maritime region of particular beauty and isolataton. There is, however, nothing foreign or narrowly "regional" about *The Lost Salt Gift of Blood*; reading MacLeod, one is led to think of the kindred worlds of Frank O'Connor's and Edna O'Brien's Ireland, A.E. Coppard's vanished England, the doomed Midlands of D.H. Lawrence. One thinks too of those extraordinary watercolours of Winslow Homer that take for their specific subjects the people and seascapes of Prout's Neck, Maine, and Cullercoats, England. To suggest that the mythic human drama defines itself by way of such localized, precisely rendered worlds is in a sense to state what is obvious – when one is speaking of art of the highest quality. But in contemplating the work at hand one is likely to forget such generalizations in the sheer urgency of the experience.

Consider the openings of MacLeod's stories: " 'We'll just have to sell him,' I remember my mother saying with finality" ("In the Fall"); "There are times even now, when I awake at four o'clock in the morning with the terrible fear that I have overslept; when I imagine that my father is waiting for me in the room below the darkened stairs"

("The Boat"); "I am speaking now of a July in the early 1970's" ("The Road to Rankin's Point"). And with what authority and ease the natural world enters the world of narrative dialectics by way of MacLeod's limpid prose: "Now in the early evening the sun is flashing everything in gold. It bathes the blunt grey rocks that loom yearningly out toward Europe and it touches upon the stunted spruce and the low-lying lichens and the delicate hardy ferns and the ganglia-rooted moss and the tiny tough rock cranberries. The grey and slanting rain squalls have swept in from the sea and then departed with all the suddenness of surprise marauders" ("The Lost Salt Gift of Blood"). This is an art that conceals itself, an employment of language so refined, yet so marvelously colloquial in its rhythms, that one is apt to forget that it *is* art, and not a blunt transcribing of life nearly, at times, too candid to be borne.

Because MacLeod is so natural a storyteller, so clearly an heir of what might be called the "oral tradition," it should be noted that this writerly vision has evolved by way of such masters as Hardy, Lawrence, Joyce, Hemingway, Faulkner (the young Joyce of *Dubliners*, that is, and the young Hemingway of *In Our Time*). He so skilfully employs the present tense ("On the twenty-eighth day of June, 1960, which is the planned day of my deliverance, I awake at exactly six A.M. to find myself on my eighteenth birthday" ["The Vastness of the Dark"]) that it is never obtrusive but works, as Joyce Cary argued, to give to the reader that sudden feeling of insecurity that comes to a traveller in unmapped country; a sense of immediacy, cinematic in its vividness.

The Lost Salt Gift of Blood contains seven stories, and it took seven years for them to be written. This is to confirm our sense that there is nothing in the volume at hand that has not been deliberated at length; nothing written in haste, or for ephemeral purposes. Virtually all of these stories, one feels, might be expanded into novels, and, indeed, they give the satisfying sense of being part of a large, generous, imaginative whole, not mere fragments. The voice varies from story to story, but it is recognizably the same voice, addressing us from out of the same authorial consciousness.

These are tales of ritual-like initiation and sacrifice. In one, a child realizes adult complicity in death; in another, a young man comes to terms with the meaning of "manhood" and the connections, radiating outward like the tendrils of a living organism, between himself and his blood kin. In still another, a young man living far from Cape Breton feels himself both isolated and defined by his father's sacrifice for him. If I were to name a single underlying motive for MacLeod's fiction, I would say that it is the urge to memorialize, the urge to sanctify. This is a sense both primitive and "modernist" that if one sets down the right words in the right, talismanic order, the purely finite and local is transcended and the voiceless is given a voice. Ballads that link the living with their Scottish ancestors are sung by wholly unself-conscious men and women. They are likely to be accompanied by a boy like John who, in the collection's title story, seems "as all mouth-organ players the world over: his right foot tapping out the measures and his small shoulders now round and hunched above the cupped hand instrument." What is passing is the more urgently prized, as poets and writers of fiction have always known, from Hardy to Yeats to Joyce to MacLeod and his fellow Cape Bretoner D.R. Mac-Donald, another gifted elegist of the contemporary Maritimes.

In such fiction, with its autobiographical nuances and authority, the narrator is often a witness. And the reader, by way of the narrator, becomes a witness. In "In the Fall," we participate not only in the child-narrator's shock at the death of a cherished horse but in the child-narrator's doomed rebelliousness against the intransigent facts of life (and death) that that horse symbolizes. In "The Boat," that most appallingly beautiful of stories, the father in dying is memorialized in such incantatory prose –

neither is it easy to know that your father was found on November twenty-eighth, ten miles to the north and wedged between two boulders at the base of the rock-strewn cliffs where he had been hurled and slammed so many many times. His hands were shredded ribbons as were his feet which had lost their boots to the suction of the sea, and his shoulders came apart in our hands when we tried to move him from the rocks. And the fish had eaten his testicles and the gulls had pecked out his eyes and the white-green stubble of his whiskers had continued to grow in death, like the grass on graves, upon the purple, bloated mass that was his face. There was not much left of my father, physically, as he lay there with the brass chains on his wrists and the seaweed in his hair.

– that the reader is made to understand he is no solitary man; his sacrifice of himself (he who was never suited to be a fisherman, nor ever wanted to be one!) no solitary sacrifice. One is reminded of the ancient English and Scottish ballads, in which the motive to preserve, to honour, to celebrate, to mourn and bear witness took the form of song.

In Alistair MacLeod's short stories, one encounters the narrator as son and brother but above all as witness: embarked upon a life's enterprise of forging not the conscience of his race, like young Stephen Dedalus, but being the means by which its conscience is expressed. For thoughts that lie too deep for tears, as we know, are not the sole province of those who can express them. I have always considered the term "regional literature" misleading as well as condescending. Isn't fiction set in our world capitals (London, New York City, Paris, Tokyo, Toronto) regional literature in the most literal sense? Doesn't it depend for its power, if it has power, on the specifics of streets, neighbourhoods, the vagaries of local accents and local weather, the contours of landscape its inhabitants take to be permanent, and of enduring significance? In this sense all literature is regional; or, conversely, no literature is regional. Alistair MacLeod's Cape Breton is everywhere. And immediately accessible to us.

BY ALISTAIR MACLEOD

FICTION
The Lost Salt Gift of Blood (1976)
As Birds Bring Forth the Sun and Other Stories (1986)

Acknowledgements

The selections in this volume originally appeared in the following periodicals, to which grateful acknowledgement is due:

In the Fall: *Tamarack Review*, October 1973.

The Vastness of the Dark: *The Fiddlehead*, Winter 1971.

The Lost Salt Gift of Blood: *The Southern Review*, Winter 1974; *Best American Short Stories,* 1975.

The Return: *The Atlantic Advocate*, November 1971.

The Golden Gift of Grey: *Twigs* VII, 1971.

The Boat: *The Massachusetts Review*, 1968; *Best American Short Stories*, 1969.

The Road to Rankin's Point: *Tamarack Review*, Winter 1976.

New Canadian Library
The Best of Canadian Writing

NCL — A Series Worth Collecting

New Canadian Library
The Best of Canadian Writing

NCL — A Series Worth Collecting

New Canadian Library
The Best of Canadian Writing

NCL — A Series Worth Collecting

New Canadian Library
The Best of Canadian Writing

NCL — A Series Worth Collecting

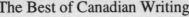

New Canadian Library
The Best of Canadian Writing

NCL — A Series Worth Collecting